If These **WALLS** *Could* **TALK:**

OAKLAND A's

*Stories from the
Oakland A's Dugout,
Locker Room, and Press Box*

Ken Korach and Susan Slusser

Library of Congress Cataloging-in-Publication Data

Names: Korach, Ken, author. | Slusser, Susan, author.
Title: Oakland A's : stories from the Oakland A's dugout, locker room, and press box / Ken Korach and Susan Slusser.
Description: Chicago, Illinois : Triumph Books LLC, [2018] | Series: If these walls could talk
Identifiers: LCCN 2018043423 | ISBN 9781629375809 (paperback)
Subjects: LCSH: Oakland Athletics (Baseball team)—History—Anecdotes. | BISAC: SPORTS & RECREATION / Baseball / General. | TRAVEL / United States / West / Pacific (AK, CA, HI, NV, OR, WA).
Classification: LCC GV875.O24 K67 2018 | DDC 796.357/640979466—dc23
LC record available at https://lccn.loc.gov/2018043423

This book is available in quantity at special discounts for your group or organization. For further information, contact:
Triumph Books LLC
814 North Franklin Street
Chicago, Illinois 60610
(312) 337–0747
www.triumphbooks.com

Printed in U.S.A.

ISBN: 978-1-62937-580-9

Design by Amy Carter

In memory of Frances Korach
and Richard Slusser

CONTENTS

CHAPTER ONE

IT IS WRITTEN IN THE ANCIENT BOOKS that when visiting a man who is soon to die, one must carry the knotted rope of elephant tail.

So when the uniformed guard told him that the President would see him now, Vice President Asiphar waited until the guard had left, and then secreted the bulky knot in the right back pocket of his uniform trousers. Only then did he walk from his own office and follow the guard down the hall, the sounds of their heels clicking on the marble floor, the only rupture in the monumental stillness of the ornate palace.

Asiphar paused outside the carved, double-oak doors, took a deep breath and then pulled open the heavy door. He stepped inside, allowed the door to shut behind him, and looked up.

The President of Scambia was standing at the window, looking out over the grounds that surrounded the palace. The palace itself had been built of blue slatelike stones that were mined in the small and still new country; the grounds reflected the President's preoccupation with blue.

They were crisscrossed in mazes of pools and gardens and hedges. The water in the pools was blue, so were the flowers — even the precisely cut hedges were of so deep a green as to appear blue.

The uniforms of the palace guards were blue, too, and the President noted that fact with satisfaction. It would be the nation's tradition.

1

When a nation is nothing — has nothing — tradition is not a bad place to begin building.

The only mar to the color scheme of the palace was the yellow of the uniforms of the work crew laying a sewer under the roadway, at the corner of the east wing of the palace building. It annoyed the President to see it, as it had annoyed him every day for the four weeks the crew had been working. But he would say nothing. A nation must have sewers as well as tradition.

President Dashiti turned now, to face the man who stood across the desk from him. During the interview, he would find it necessary to turn to the window from time to time, so as not to commit the discourtesy of smiling openly at the uniform Vice President Asiphar wore. It was of red gabardine, and every available inch of seam appeared to be trimmed with braid: gold braid, silver braid, blue and white braid. The uniform had been tailored in Paris, but not even its immaculate tailoring could disguise the obesity of Vice President Asiphar.

Not that many noticed, on first meeting, that Asiphar was fat. The first impression always was that he was ugly. More striking than his hideous uniforms, more impressive than his enormous bulk, was his face — a blue-black inkwell of darkness. His nose was wide, his forehead sloped back to a pointed head, that, fortunately, was hidden by his braided military cap.

President Dashiti once had wrestled for three weeks in his own mind, trying to determine if Asiphar looked more like a circus fat man or an out-of-shape Neanderthal. The body belonged to the circus, the face to prehistoric man. The question had been left unresolved.

More important was the fact that Asiphar was a military man, the choice of the generals for vice president, and it was necessary to tolerate him, no matter how loathsome Dashiti found him.

But toleration was not trust, and the President gave himself full approval to distrust Vice President Asiphar. How could one not distrust a man who spent twenty-four hours a day perspiring? Even now rivulets of sweat ran down the vice president's face, and the backs of his hands glistened with pearl drops of perspiration. They were here together, not under strain or tension, but merely to discuss Asiphar's vacation plans.

"Be sure," the President said, "to visit the Russian embassy. Then, of course, stop in at the American embassy. And let them know you have been to the Russian embassy."

"Certainly," Asiphar said. "But why?"

"Because this will surely get us more guns from the Russians and more money from the Americans."

Vice President Asiphar made no effort to hide his distaste; involuntarily, his right hand moved to his hip and his fingertips felt the knotted elephant tail in his pocket.

"You disapprove, general?"

"It is not my place to approve or disapprove, my president," Asiphar said. His voice was thick and guttural, his accent guaranteed that he had not been schooled at Sandhurst. "It is just that I am not comfortable living on the largesse of other nations."

President Dashiti sighed and sank slowly into his soft, blue leather chair. Only then did Asiphar sit down across the desk from him.

"Nor am I, general," Dashiti said. "But there is little else we can do. We are called an emerging nation. Yet, you know as I, that we have emerged from barbarism to backwardness. We will have many years to rule, before our people can live from the fruits of their own productivity."

He paused, as if inviting an answer, then went on.

"We were not lucky enough to have oil. Only that accursed blue stone, and how much of that could we sell? How long would our people live off that? But we have something more important. Our location. Here on this island, we control the Mozambique Channel and thus much of the world's shipping and so does whichever great power we happen to side with. And so our course is clear. We side with none; we talk with all, and we accept their largesse until that day when it will no longer be necessary. But until that day comes, we must play the game, and so you must visit their embassies on your stay in Switzerland."

He picked delicately at the crease of his shadow-striped white suit, and then his shrewd eyes raised to meet the cow-eyes of Asiphar across the desk.

"Of course, I shall, my president," Asiphar said. "And now, with your permission?"

"Certainly," Dashiti said, rising to his feet and extending his slim tan hand which was alone in air, for just a fraction of a second, before being engulfed in Asiphar's blubbery black fingers. "Have an enjoyable vacation," Dashiti said. "I wish I were going with you." He smiled, with real warmth, and tried to hide his revulsion at Asiphar's sweaty hand.

The two men held the handshake, their eyes locked together, then Asiphar turned away. The President released his hand, and with a slight bow, Asiphar turned and walked across the carpeted floor to the twelve-foot high doors.

He did not smile until he was past the two blue-uniformed guards who stood watch outside the President's office door. But he smiled on his way down the hall to the elevator. He smiled in the elevator. And he smiled while walking to his chauffeured Mercedes-Benz limousine, parked in front of the palace. He sank back into the soft cushions of the rear seat, breathing deeply of the dry, air-conditioned coolness. Then, still smiling, he told his chauffeur: "The airport."

The car slowly made its way out, along the circular drive in front of the palace. The driver slowed, to inch past the half-dozen yellow-suited workmen, digging a deep excavation next to the east wing wall of the palace, and muttered a curse under his breath. Aloud, he said, "These fools seem to have been digging for months."

Asiphar was too pleased with himself to worry about the laggard performance of workmen, so he said nothing. The knot in his right hip pocket pressed uncomfortably against his flesh. He pulled it from his pocket and held it in his hands, looking at it, feeling the toughness of the hide, beginning to plan the remarks he would make upon his ascension to the presidency in just seven more days. Asiphar. The president of Scambia.

President Dashiti stood by the window, watching Asiphar's limousine slow down while passing the sewer-diggers, then speed up as it neared the nation's only paved road, leading from the palace to the airport.

One should never trust generals, he thought. They think only about obtaining power. They never think of exercising power. How fortunate that we entrust to them only unimportant things like wars. He turned back toward his desk, to study and then to sign requests by his nation for more foreign aid.

Asiphar, at that moment, was thinking of the time, only a few days hence, when Scambia would no longer need aid from any nation. We will be the greatest power of all, he thought, and our flag will be respected and feared by every nation.

No power can stop me, he thought. No power; neither government nor man.

CHAPTER TWO

HIS NAME WAS REMO and he felt foolish wearing the coarse brown monk's robe. The knotted cord hung heavily around his waist and he considered for a moment that it might be a good tool to strangle someone with. Not that Remo used tools.

He stood now in front of the West Side Federal Penitentiary, waiting for the big metal door to open. The palms of his hands were sweaty. He wiped them on the brown robe and realized that he could not remember the last time he had perspired. It was the heavy robe, he told himself, then called himself a liar and admitted he was sweating because he was standing outside a penitentiary, waiting to go inside. He again jabbed the small button on the right side of the door, and through the thick glass window, he could see the guard looking up at him, an annoyed expression on his face.

Then the guard pushed a button on his desk, the door shuddered, and began to chug back slowly, an inch at a time, like a roller coaster reaching the top of a hill. It opened only about twenty inches and stopped, so Remo had to turn sideways to get his broad shoulders through the narrow opening. As he passed, he could see that the door was two inches thick, all metal. He was barely inside when he heard the door begin to bang shut behind him, closing finally with a dungeon-door-sound thump.

He was in a reception room and the eyes of a half dozen black women, waiting for visiting hours, went to his face. He wondered if he should lower the cowl that shrouded his face. He left it up. He approached the thick bulletproof glass, enclosing the guard's desk and leaned against the glass. It was solid under his hands and he gauged its thickness at precisely one inch. It would take a powerful weapon to penetrate that glass, even at close range.

Without looking up, the guard flicked a lever, again double-locking the front door. If Remo had to get out in a hurry, he would go through the glass, and through the door behind the guard. Remo rapped on the glass with the heel of his hand, getting the feel of its weight, and the guard moved his head, motioning to Remo to pick up the telephone that stood on a small shelf in front of him.

Remo picked it up and tried to keep his voice calm. "I'm Father Tuck," he said, restraining a smirk. "I have an appointment with the prisoner Devlin."

"Just a minute, Father," the guard said, setting down the telephone with infuriating slowness. Casually, he began looking down a typewritten list of names, until he came to one that Remo, upside down, could read:

"DEVLIN, BERNARD. FATHER TUCK."

The guard turned the sheet of paper over and picked up the telephone again.

"Okay, Father," he said. "That door over there." With his head, he nodded toward another door in the corner of the room.

"Thank you, my son," Remo said.

He followed the guard's directions to another metal door. It was ceiling high and six feet wide. A painted sign on it said "push," but the sign was fresh and unscarred, while the bars above it were worn, where thousands of people had placed their hands to push.

Remo had held bars before. He placed his palms against the sign and he could feel a small electric pulse as a switch released the electric lock. He pressed forward and the door opened slowly.

The door swung shut behind him and he was in another small room. To his right, behind more bulletproof glass, was a mesh cage where three prisoners sat waiting to be released, watched by another guard. Again he heard the door thud shut behind him.

To his left, a door led to a stairway. He pushed against that door, but it did not give. He glanced back over his shoulder. The guard was talking to one of the prisoners. Remo walked over and rapped on the window. The guard looked up, nodded, then pushed a button. Remo went back, pushed open the door, and entered the stairwell. It was a narrow flight of stairs, and the risers were higher than normal. At the bottom of the stairs, a mirror was angled against the wall, and as he went up the stairs, he saw an identical mirror set in the corner of the wall at the head of the stairs. He glanced up into that mirror and then back down, off the bottom mirror and out to the desk where the guard sat. From his post, the guard could see the entire stairway. There was no way to hide there, no bannisters to climb upon, no ledge to wedge oneself on.

He walked up the stairs, exercising, kicking with his bare toes against the robe, swirling it forward so that his foot could step up to the next step without tripping on the robe. He tried not to remember going up the same kind of narrow stairway to a death cell ten years earlier.

No use. The sweat came like a flow. His armpits were wet.

Ten years ago.

Life was simpler then. He was Remo Williams. Patrolman Remo Williams, Newark P.D. A good cop. Then someone had killed a drug pusher in an alley on his beat and he was convicted and sentenced to an electric chair that didn't work right.

What the hell am I doing here? At the top of the stairs, there was another door. Just as there had been in the death house in the New Jersey State Prison. Uninvited, more memories of that invaded his mind. The visit from the monk, the black pill, the metal helmet on his head and then seventy-seven zillion volts that were supposed to go through his body to kill him, but didn't.

He was in the next room now and there was an old wooden desk. Behind it sat a uniformed guard, wearing a name tag that read Wm. O'Brien. He was a medium-sized man and Remo noticed one of his arms was shorter than the other. Big knobby wrists stuck out of his blue uniform shirt. His eyes were small and washed-out blue, his nose bulbous with broken blood vessels around the sides and tip.

"I'm Father Tuck. I've come to see the prisoner Devlin."

"Why so hot, Father?" O'Brien asked.

Remo did not answer. Then, he said, "Devlin, please."

O'Brien was very slow getting up from his chair and he looked the priest over carefully, with shrewd eyes, looking past the brown robe — convincing himself that this man was no priest at all. His hands were roughened along the sides of the palms, but his fingernails were manicured and his cuticles formed perfect crescents.

The monk also exuded the aroma of expensive aftershave lotion which was definitely unpriestly, although O'Brien did not know that it was a special French brand named P.C. for "Post-Coitus." O'Brien glanced down as he stepped from behind the desk. The monk's feet seemed to be too clean, and even his toenails had colorless nail polish on them.

Definitely not a priest. O'Brien had been casual about the inspection, but Remo had noticed it and anticipated his conclusion. Damn. Now if there was trouble, two would have to go.

O'Brien said nothing. He took Remo into a small wood-paneled conference room and politely asked him to wait. He disappeared through another door and five minutes later returned with a man in tow.

"Sit down, Devlin," he said.

Devlin sat down easily, in a bare wooden chair facing the monk. He was a tall, thin man and the blue prison clothes fit him as if they had been tailored. His hair was black and wavy, and his skin color told of frequent trips to the islands, perhaps membership in a very good health club."

He looked to be about thirty years old and his confident posture, the small laughter crinkles around intelligently flashing eyes, testified that he had enjoyed every minute of those thirty years. Up until now.

Remo sat silently, waiting for O'Brien to leave. Then the guard went through the doorway leading back to his desk.

"Knock, Father, when you're done," he said, and pulled the door tight behind him. Remo heard the lock snap shut.

He put a finger to his lips and walked softly to the door, squatting down to peer through the keyhole. He could see O'Brien's back, again seated at his desk.

Only then did Remo sit down and address Devlin:

"All right. Let's have it," he said.

9

He tried to concentrate while Devlin talked, but found it difficult. All he could think of was the penitentiary and how he wanted to be out of it. Even more, perhaps, than ten years ago, when he had been saved from the electric chair by a secret governmental organization with a Presidential crime-fighting mission, so he could be trained to be its killer arm. Code name: Destroyer.

Bits and pieces of Devlin's talk broke through his reverie. The African nation of Scambia. A plan to turn it into an international refuge for criminals from all over the world. The president to be assassinated; the vice president to take his place.

Bored, because information-gathering was not his specialty. Remo tried to think of questions to ask.

Who's behind it all?

I don't know.

The vice president? This Asiphar?

No. I don't think so.

How did you find out about it?

I work for a man in this country who has an interest in this sort of thing. That's how I know. I did some legal research for him on extradition laws.

I know your reputation as the big Mafia lawyer, getting thugs out of jail on technicalities.

Everybody's entitled to a defense.

And now you're spilling, so you get a break? Remo was disgusted with him.

Yes. I'm spilling so I get out of here and I get safe conduct some place. "And I'll tell you the truth, Father," he said, sneering the title, "I'm getting tired of telling my story to every nit the government sends through the door."

"Well, I'll be the last one," Remo said. He got up and went to the door again, peering through the keyhole.

O'Brien still sat at his desk, now reading a newspaper, his broad back rising slowly with his breathing. A radio played softly alongside O'Brien's desk.

"Okay, then," Devlin said. "How do I get out of here? Do I call a press conference or what?"

"No, that's not necessary," Remo said. "We've got it all worked out."

Remo knew what he had to do. His hand shook slightly as he pulled the wooden crucifix from a pocket in the billowing robe and showed it to Devlin. "See here," he said, pointing with his left hand. "That black pill at the bottom of the feet. When the guard comes in, kiss the cross, and nip the pill off with your teeth. When you're back in your cell, bite into it and swallow it. It'll knock you out. Our men are in the prison hospital now. When they bring you in, they'll decide you need special treatment. Put you in an ambulance and send you to a private hospital. The ambulance will never get there. Neither will you."

"Sounds too easy," Devlin said. "I don't think it'll work."

"Man, it's worked a hundred times for me," Remo said. "Think this is the first time I've done this? You're going to live for a thousand years."

He stood up. "I'm going to call the guard now," Remo said. "We've been here too long."

He went to the wooden door and pounded on it with the side of his hand. The loud thump echoed and reverberated through the small room. The door opened and O'Brien stood there.

"Thank you," Remo said. He turned to Devlin who sat still on his seat. He extended the crucifix to him and shielded O'Brien's view with his body. "God bless you, my son," he said.

Devlin didn't move. Bite it off, goddam you, Remo thought. Otherwise, I'll have to kill you right here. And O'Brien, too.

He shoved the crucifix closer to Devlin's face.

"The Lord will protect you," he said. If you don't take that pill, you're going to need the Lord. He waved the crucifix in front of Devlin, who looked at him, doubt on his finely-featured face, and then shrugged imperceptibly and reached out both hands, taking the crucifix, carrying it to his mouth, and kissing the feet of the statue.

"Eternal life will be yours," Remo said, and winked at Devlin, who did not know that for him, eternity would end in fifteen minutes.

"Can you find your way out, Father?" O'Brien asked.

"Yes," Remo answered.

"Then I'll take the prisoner back," O'Brien said. "Good day, Father."

"Good day. Good day, Mr. Devlin." Remo turned to the door, glancing down at the crucifix, noting with relief that the black pill had gone. Devlin was a dead man. Good.

He could not resist the challenge. At the top of the stairs, he waited until the guard downstairs had looked up into the reflecting mirror to check the staircase. Then, hitching up his robe, Remo moved into the narrow stairwell, his body skittering from side to side, his feet moving noiselessly down the steps. The guard looked, unconcerned, into the staircase mirror again, and Remo broke his rhythm, melting into a vague shadow-shape on the wall. The guard looked down again at his papers.

Remo coughed. The guard looked up, startled to see someone there.

"Oh, Father? I didn't see you come down."

"No," Remo agreed pleasantly. It took three more minutes for him to get through the penitentiary's infallible security system.

He was soaked with perspiration by the time he reentered the bright sunshine of the day, and he was in such a hurry to get distance between himself and the prison that he did not bother to notice the two men across the street, who matched their pace to his and followed him at a leisurely gait.

CHAPTER THREE

REMO PUSHED THROUGH THE REVOLVING door of the Palazzo Hotel, then stepped quickly across the marble lobby, toward a bank of elevators in the corner.

A bellhop leaned against a small counter, watching him. As Remo stood by the elevators, he came up alongside.

"Sorry, Father," he said briskly, "no panhandling."

Remo smiled gently. "I've come, my son, to perform last rites."

"Oh," the pimply-faced bellhop said, disappointed that his show of power had failed. "Who's dead?"

"You will be if you don't get your ugly, bugging face out of my way," Remo said. The bellhop looked at him, this time carefully, and the monk was no longer smiling gently. The face was hard and angular; the expression would have shattered crystal. The bellhop got his face out of there.

Remo rode the elevator to the eleventh floor, giving a blessing to an old woman who entered on the seventh floor and got out on the eighth. Then he was in the hallway on the eleventh floor, heading for one of the expensive suites on the left side of the corridor.

He paused outside the door, heard the usual mélange of voices from inside, and with a small sigh unlocked the door and stepped in.

At the end of a small hallway was a living room. From the doorway, Remo could see the back of an aged Oriental, seated in a lotus position on the floor, his eyes riveted to a television set whose picture was pale and washed out in the bright noontime sun.

The man did not move as Remo entered the room. He did not speak.

Remo walked up behind him until he was only a foot away. He leaned over, close to the man's head, and then shouted at the top of his voice:

"Hello, Chiun."

Not a muscle moved; not a nerve reacted. Then — slowly — the Oriental's head lifted and in the mirror over the television, his eyes met Remo's. He lowered his eyes to Remo's brown robes, then said, "You will find the Salvation Army mission in the next street." He returned his eyes to the television set, playing forth its daytime drama of tragedy and suffering.

Remo shrugged and went into his bedroom to change. He was worried about Chiun. He had known the deadly little Korean for ten years now, ever since Chiun had been given the assignment by CURE to make Remo Williams the perfect human weapon. In those years, he had seen Chiun do things that defied belief. He had seen him smash his hand through walls, walk up the sides of buildings, destroy death machines, wipe out platoons of men, all by the strange harnessing of power in that frail eighty year old body.

But now, Remo feared, that body was running down, and with it, Chiun's spirit. He no longer seemed to care. He showed less interest in his training sessions with Remo. He seemed less anxious to cook a meal, to make sure that he and Remo were not poisoned by the dealers in dog meat who called themselves restaurateurs. He had even stopped his incessant lecturing and scolding of Remo. It seemed that all he wanted to do was to sit in front of the television and watch soap operas.

No doubt about it, Remo thought, as he peeled off the brown robe, uncovering nylon lavender briefs and undershirt. He's slipping. Well, why not? He's eighty years old. Shouldn't he slip?

It was all very logical, but what did it have to do with a force of nature? It was like saying the rain was slipping.

But he was slipping nevertheless. Yet, for the better part of those eighty years, Chiun had plied his trade very well. Better than any man before. Better, perhaps, than any man would ever do again. If there were a hall of fame for assassins, the central display belonged to Chiun. They could stick everybody else, Remo Williams included, in an outside alley.

Remo rolled the monk's robe up into a brown ball, wrapped it tightly with its own white rope, and dropped it into a wastepaper basket. From a wall-length closet, he took out a pair of mustard-colored slacks and put them on. Then a light blue sports shirt. He kicked off the sandals and slid his feet into slip-on canvas boat-shoes.

He splashed skin-bracer on his face and neck, then walked back into the living room.

The telephone was ringing. Chiun studiously ignored it.

It would be Smith, the one, the only — thank God, the only — Dr. Harold W. Smith, head of CURE.

Remo picked up the telephone.

"Palazzo Monastery," he said.

The lemony voice whined at him. "Don't be a smartass, Remo." Then, "And why are you staying at the Palazzo?"

"There was no room at the inn," Remo said. "Besides, you're paying for it. Therefore it gives me pleasure."

"Oh, you're very funny today," Smith said, and Remo could picture him twirling his thirty-nine-cent plastic letter opener and magnifying glass at his desk at Folcroft Sanitarium, the headquarters for CURE.

"Well, I don't feel funny," Remo growled. "I'm supposed to be on vacation, not running errands for some..."

Smith interrupted him. "Before you get abusive, put on the scrambler, please."

"Yeah, sure," Remo said. He put down the telephone and opened the drawer of the small end-table. In it were two plastic, foam-covered cylinders that resembled space-age earmuffs. Remo picked up one of them, looked at the back of it for identification, then snapped it on the earpiece of the phone. He snapped the other over the mouthpiece.

"Okay, they're on," he said. "Can I shout now?"

"Not yet," Smith said. "First set the dials on the back to number fourteen. Remember to set each one of them to fourteen. And then turn the units on. That's important too."

"Up yours," Remo mumbled as he held the telephone away from

15

him and set the dials on the back of the scrambler units. It was CURE's latest invention. A portable telephone scrambler system that defied interception, recording devices, and nosy switchboard operators.

Then Remo flicked the "on" switches and raised the phone back to his ear.

"All right," he said. "I'm ready."

All he heard was garble, as if a man were gargling.

"I got it set," Remo shouted. "What the hell's wrong now?"

"Grrgle. Grrble. Drrble. Frgle."

Remo regarded it as an improvement over what Smith generally had to say.

"Grrgle. Frppp."

"Yes," Remo said. "In your hat."

"Grggle. Drbble."

"Yes. And put your foot in it. Up to your ankle."

"Brggle. Cringle."

"And your Aunt Millie too." Remo said sweetly.

Then Smith's voice broke in. "Remo. Are you there?" His voice was clear, but slightly brittle.

"Well, of course I'm here. Where else would I be?"

"Sorry. I had trouble with the device."

"Fire the inventor. Better yet, kill him. That's your answer to everything anyway. Now, as I was saying, about my vacation."

"Forget your vacation," Smith said. "Tell me about Devlin. What did he have to say?"

"That is about my vacation," Remo said. "You called me in to talk to him, when it's not a problem for us. It belongs to the CIA. So why the hell don't you give it to the CIA? Empire-building again?"

"No," said Smith, petulantly, wondering why he felt any need to explain anything to Remo who was, after all, only a hired hand. "The fact is that the CIA questioned Devlin three times. Three different agents. All three were killed. In fact, I was going to tell you to be careful."

"Thanks for telling me," Remo said.

"I figured it wouldn't matter," Smith said. "Now what did Devlin say?"

Remo recounted the story, the plan to assassinate the President of

Scambia, to set the small nation up as a haven for the world's criminals, the implicating of the Vice President, Alibaba, or something...

"Asiphar," Smith interrupted.

"Yeah, Asiphar. Anyway, he's in it, but he's not the leader. Devlin didn't know the leader."

"When is it scheduled to happen?"

"In a week," Remo said. Deep inside his stomach, he felt that first small tinge that unfailingly told him of impending catastrophes, such as the necessity to postpone his vacation.

"Mmmmm," Smith mused. Then he was silent. Then "mmmmm" again.

"Don't bother telling me what 'mmmm' means. I know," Remo said.

"This is serious, Remo, very serious."

"Yeah? Why?"

"Have you ever heard of Baron Isaac Nemeroff?"

"Sure. I buy all my shirts from him."

Smith ignored him. "Nemeroff is probably the most dangerous criminal in the world today. He has a houseguest this week at his villa in Algeria."

"Do I get three guesses?"

"You don't need any," Smith said. "It's Vice President Asiphar of Scambia."

"So?" Remo said.

"So, that means, that Nemeroff is involved in this. Probably the man who started it. And that is very dangerous."

"All right. Assume everything you say is true," Remo lectured. "It's still a job for the CIA."

"Thank you for your lecture on policy," Smith sniffed. "Now let me tell you something. You seem to have forgotten our basic mission which is to fight crime. That effort will be seriously compromised if Nemeroff and Asiphar are allowed to make this Scambia a haven for criminals."

Remo paused. "So I'm elected?"

"You're elected."

"And what about my vacation?"

"Your vacation?" Smith said loudly. "All right, if you insist upon talking about it, let's discuss vacations. How many weeks a year do you think you're entitled to?"

"With my longevity, at least four," Remo said.

"All right. Where did you spend three weeks of last month?"

"In San Juan, but I was training," Remo said. "I've got to keep in shape."

"All right," Smith said. "But the four weeks you spent in Buenos Aires, in a damned chess tournament? That was training too, I suppose."

"Certainly, it was," Remo said indignantly. "I've got to keep my wits razor-sharp."

"Do you think it was sharp-witted to enter the tournament under the name of Paul Morphy?" Smith said coldly.

"It was the only way I could get a game with Fischer."

"Oh, yes, that game. You spotted him pawn and move, I believe," Smith said.

"Yeah, and I would have beat him too if I hadn't gotten careless and let him capture my queen on the sixth move," Remo said, annoyed to even have to remember the business in Buenos Aires, which had not been one of his brighter moments. "Look," he said hurriedly. "You're too upset now to talk about things like vacations. Suppose I do this job and then we'll talk about vacations? What do you say?"

What Smith said was, "I'll get a file to you. Everything we know. Perhaps something will come out of it. But about all this vacation time..."

Remo turned the dial on the earpiece from fourteen to twelve and immediately Smith's voice went berserk again.

"Grbble, breek, gleeble."

"I'm sorry, Doctor Smith, we're having trouble again with this de —" Remo turned the dial on the mouthpiece to another setting. He could picture Smith at Folcroft, furiously twisting the dials, trying to get Remo's voice back.

Into the mouthpiece, Remo said: "Brueghel, Rommel, Stein and Hinderbeck. Sausage meat machines. Cold cuts, one dollar the pound, up to your ankle. Don't make no bull moves, Dutch Schultz." He hung up. Let Smith chew on that one for awhile.

As he removed the scrambler units from the phone, he tried not to feel his annoyance. He didn't need a file from Smith. He didn't need any neat computer printouts. All he needed was the description and location of the targets. Nemeroff. Asiphar. They were dead. That was that. Girl scouts could do it. A stupid thing to let louse up a vacation.

Remo put the scrambler units back in the drawer, kicked off his tennis shoes and watched the back of Chiun's head. He wanted to tell Chiun about his feelings today at the federal prison. How he had been frightened and nervous, almost out of control.

He wanted to tell him. It was important. He hoped a commercial would come soon.

He lay there, waiting for one. But if I tell Chiun, what? Will he lecture me? Give me exercises to do? Tell me that white men can never control their feelings?

Maybe, a year ago, he would. But now? Probably, he just wouldn't be interested. He'd just grunt and keep staring at the television.

Remo did not want that to happen. He decided not to tell Chiun.

CHAPTER FOUR

"C'MON, YOU WANT TO GO to the zoo?"

The old man had turned off the television and was beginning to hook up his TV tape player to play back the shows he had missed because of concurrent scheduling.

Even his white robe seemed to rise in indignation as he looked at Remo, then answered softly:

"This is all a zoo. All the place, all around the place. No, thank you. But you go. Perhaps you can teach the bull moose how to bellow."

Remo shrugged and disguised a sigh. There was no doubt about it. He was not the same Chiun any longer. The Master of Sinanju was growing old, but somehow it seemed obscene that that finely-honed weapon, the only person Remo had ever loved, should be subject to growing old. As if he were a mere mortal. As if he were not the Master of Sinanju.

Remo got up to leave but paused at the door. "Chiun, can I bring you anything back? A newspaper? A book?"

"If there is a special on arteries somewhere, buy me five feet. Otherwise nothing." Then he was back in his lotus position, again staring at the set, and Remo could not remember ever feeling so sad.

If the two men in the lobby had worn neon sandwich boards, they could not have been more obvious. They sat on the edge of two facing chairs, their heads leaned forward, talking to each other. Each time the elevator door opened, they looked up and then, finding nothing of interest, put their heads back together. When Remo came out of the elevator, their eyes locked on him and they nodded at each other, imperceptibly.

Remo spotted them as soon as the elevator door opened. His first instinct placed them as cops, but why cops should be eyeing him, he couldn't understand. Maybe they were just plain thugs. The two groups were usually indistinguishable, generally coming from the same social class.

Without appearing to watch them, he saw them eye him, he saw them nod to each other, he saw them get up from their chairs and walk around to intercept him near the door. He was not going to be grabbed by them outside. If they wanted to talk to him, they could use the lobby.

So Remo walked to the cigar stand and bought a pack of True Blues. Maybe he'd have one later. He had not smoked a cigarette in a year. He picked up a copy of the afternoon *Post*, which read like the Tel Aviv edition of the *National Enquirer*, and gave the old lady at the stand a dollar and told her to keep the change.

He folded the paper lengthwise, stood against a wall next to a potted palm and began to read the main sports story on the back page. He would outwait them.

He hadn't long to wait. The two men sidled up to him and Remo decided they were not policemen; they moved too well.

Both were tall. One was Italian-looking and lean. The other was burly, his skin tended toward yellow and there was a trace of the epicanthic fold over his eyes. Remo thought, Hawaiian maybe, Polynesian somehow. Both men had the same kind of eyes, humorless, somehow always connected with the profession of crime — either solving it or committing it.

Remo knew the eyes well. He saw them every morning when he shaved.

He felt something pressed against his side, just above the right hip, something hard.

"I know," he said, "don't do anything stupid, I've got a gun stuck in my ribs."

The Hawaiian, or whatever — who held the gun — smiled. "Smart guy, are you? That's good. Then we won't have to tell you anything twice."

The other man took up position in front of Remo, screening him from the view of the rest of the lobby.

"What is it you want?" Remo asked.

"We want to know who you're working for." This time the Italian-looking one spoke. His voice was as brittle as his features.

"The Zingo Rollerskate and Surfboard Company," Remo said.

The gun jabbed into his ribs hard. The burly one said, "Now I thought you were going to be smart. And instead you're being stupid."

"You must have the wrong guy," Remo said. "I tell you, I work for the Zingo Rollerskate and Surfboard Company."

"And your job is to dress up like a priest and to visit jails?" the burly one asked. He was about to go on when a look from the other silenced him.

So they knew. So what? If they were cops, they would have brought him in. Since they weren't, it wasn't likely anyone was going to care much about what happened to them.

"All right," Remo said, "you got me. I'm a private detective."

"What's your name?" asked the man with the gun.

"Roger Willis."

"That's a funny name for a detective."

"It's a funny name for anyone," the Italian said.

"Did you come here to make fun of my name?" Remo said, trying to sound outraged.

"No," the Italian said. "Who are you working for?"

"He's a European," Remo said. "Some kind of Russian."

"His name?"

"Nemeroff," Remo said. "Baron Isaac Nemeroff." He watched their eyes carefully for any sign of reaction. There was none. So they were just lower-echelon goons who would know nothing, who could tell him nothing. Suddenly, he resented their wasting time which he could better spend at the zoo.

"Why'd he hire you?" the Italian said.

"I don't know. Probably let his fingers do the walking through the yellow pages. It pays to advertise. He sent me a letter. And a check."

"You still got the letter?"

"Sure. It's up in my room. Listen, pal, I don't want any trouble. This was just a simple talky-talk job. If it's more than that, just let me know and I'll get the hell out of it. I don't need any headaches."

"You be a nice boy, Roger, and you won't have any," the Hawaiian said. "Come on." He jabbed Remo with the pistol before putting it back into his pocket. "We're going up to your room to get the letter."

Remo looked at him carefully, and noticed two things. First, they planned to kill him. No doubt about it. Second, the burly one had hazel eyes. And that was interesting.

Remo was happy that they wanted to go to his room. He had wanted to get them out of the lobby, where things could get crowded and messy, causing the hotel management to complain. Smith might even hear about it.

He turned and led the way toward the elevator and calmly jabbed the up button.

When the doors opened, he stepped in first. The two men took posts on either side of him; the oriental type on his left, slightly behind him. Remo knew the pistol was pointing through his pocket at Remo's left kidney. He was really interested in those hazel eyes.

So far as he knew, only one type of oriental had hazel eyes: Koreans.

On the eleventh floor, he led them carefully down the hallway to his room. He took the key from his pocket, then stopped.

"Listen, I don't want any trouble. I don't want you to think I'm pulling a fast one. My partner is inside."

"Is he armed?" the Italian one asked.

"Armed?" Remo laughed and watched the burly one's face. "He's an eighty-year-old Korean. He was a friend of my grandfather's."

At the word Korean, the yellow-skinned man's eyes had narrowed. So he *was* Korean. Hey, Chiun, guess who's coming to dinner?

The Italian one nodded toward the door. The Korean took the key, opened the door quietly, then pushed it back. It swung open and the handle hit the door with a thud. Chiun was still seated in his white robes on the floor, watching television. He did not turn. He made no sound; he did not acknowledge the intrusion.

"That him?"

"Yeah," Remo said. "He's harmless."

"I hate Koreans," the yellow-skinned man said, his lip twisting in an involuntary rictus.

He preceded Remo into the suite. Remo was surprised at how sloppy the two of them were. Neither checked the bedrooms, the bathrooms or the closets. If he had wanted to, Remo could have hidden an Army platoon in the suite, but these two incompetents would not have known.

The one with hazel eyes stood in the middle of the living room floor, Remo behind him, the Italian behind him.

"Hey, old man," the Korean called.

Chiun did not move, but Remo saw his eyes lift in the mirror, scan the scene behind him, then lower to the television screen. Poor Chiun. A tired old man.

"Hey. I'm talking to you," the burly man roared. Chiun studiously ignored him and the big man went around in front of him and pulled the tape cartridge from the television set.

Chiun rose in the one smooth motion that always impressed Remo. Every time he tried to copy it, he wound up facing in a different direction. Chiun did it automatically. Some things never deteriorated with age.

Chiun looked at the big man. Remo realized he had seen the hazel eyes and recognized a countryman.

"Please return my television program," Chiun said, extending a hand.

The big man giggled. His face contorted in a mask of hatred and he spoke to Chiun in a babble of Korean that Remo could not understand.

Chiun let him speak, let him wear himself out, and then said, quietly, in English: "And you, you piece of dog meat, are unworthy of the blood that flows in your veins. And now, return my television program. I, the Master of Sinanju, command it."

The big man's face blanched. He said, slowly, "There ain't any Master of Sinanju."

"Fool," Chiun's voice roared. "Half-caste ape. Do not tempt me to feed my anger."

He extended his hand again for the tape cartridge.

The Korean looked at Chiun's hand, then at the tape, and then with a snarl, grabbed the plastic cartridge in both hands and snapped it in half, as if it were an ice-cream stick, and dropped the two pieces to the floor.

He hit the floor before the pieces did.

With a roar of rage, Chiun was in the air, his foot planted deep into the Korean's throat, and the big man crumpled down in a heap, his hands slowly relaxing in death.

Chiun had recoiled in the air, curving his body, so now he landed on both feet, facing Remo and the Italian, his fists curved into hand maces at his hips, his weight balanced on the balls of both feet, a pictorial study of the perfect weapon.

Remo heard the Italian gasp, then he felt the rustle of clothing as the hood went for his gun.

"Do not exert yourself, little father," Remo said. "This one is mine."

The gun came out quickly, but Remo's elbow moved even more quickly, blasting backward into the man's sternum. The bone splintered under the force and the Italian should have let out a "whoomph" of air from the impact, but he didn't because he was dying. He staggered backwards, seemingly drunk, the gun waving irrelevantly around the room, and then his eyes opened wide in a look of horror. His feet stopped moving, the hand that held the gun slowly opened, dropping it onto the floor, and then he fell, heavily, his head cracking against an open closet door, but by then it was too late for him to feel it.

Remo bowed to Chiun. China bowed back.

Remo nodded his head to the dead Korean on the floor. "I guess he wasn't impressed by your credentials."

"He was a fool," Chiun said. "Trying through hatred to punish his mother's sin with a white man. When her only sin was her execrable taste. Aah, such fools."

Then he looked at Remo and his eyes dropped sadly in a parody of helplessness. "I really feel poorly today," he said. "I am very old and very weak."

"You are very devious and very lazy, as befits the true Oriental," Remo said. "We each get rid of one."

"But look at the size of him," Chiun protested, motioning to the fallen Korean. "How could I?"

"Necessity is the mother of invention. Call MotherTruckers. They move anything."

"Insolent," Chiun said. "That my years of training have produced not a thoughtful, kindly human being but a spoiled, self-indulgent white man." It was Chiun's supreme insult.

Remo smiled. Chiun smiled. They stood there, smiling at each other, like two life-sized porcelain figures.

Then, Remo remembered something.

"Wait here," he said.

"I have an appointment with the beautician?" Chiun asked.

"Please. Just wait here."

"I will leave only if Father Time comes to claim my frail shell."

Out in the hall, Remo saw what he was looking for. An empty laundry basket stood near the freight elevator. He looked around, made sure no one was in the corridor, and pulled the empty basket back to his room.

He closed the door behind him. Chiun smiled when he saw the wheeled cart.

"Very good. Now you can handle both of them."

"Chiun, you take advantage of my basic good nature. I'm tired of picking up after you."

"It is a nothing." Then Chiun was bent down, picking up the pieces of the tape cartridge, looking at them sadly. Then he spit contemptuously at the Korean.

"So much hatred," he said.

"We contribute our share," Remo said.

"I," Chiun said, his voice plumbing the depths of hurt. "Whom do I hate?"

"Every one but Koreans," Remo said. Glancing at the burly man, he said, "And some of them too."

"That is not true. I tolerate most people. But hatred? Never."

"And me, little father? Do you tolerate me too?"

"Not you, my son. You, I love. Because you are really a Korean at heart. The kind of sturdy, brave, noble, thoughtful Korean who would clean up the mess of these two baboons."

Remo cleaned up the mess.

He put the two bodies into the laundry cart and then stripped the sheets from the sofa bed. He tossed them on top of the bodies and pushed the cart into the hall.

At the end of the hallway was the laundry chute. When he tipped up the cart, the sheets and bodies tumbled into the chute and down the slide. He waited until he heard the dull thud, far below. If the Palazzo laundry was as efficient as its room service, the bodies wouldn't be discovered for a week. He pushed the cart into a broom closet and went back to his room, whistling. He felt good. The events of the last few minutes had seemed to perk Chiun up. And that was well worth the effort.

Chiun was waiting for him, back in the room. He motioned to Remo to sit on the couch, and then he sat on the floor before Remo, looking up at him.

"You have been worried about me?" he said.

"Yes, I have, little father," Remo said. There was no point in lying. Chiun would always know. "You have seemed to be...to be losing your zest for life."

"And you worried?"

"I worried. Yes."

"For causing you that worry, I apologize," Chiun said. "Remo. I have been the Master of Sinanju for fifty years."

"None could have been finer."

"That is true," Chiun said, nodding, placing his fingertips together. "Still, it is many years."

"It is many years," Remo agreed.

"I have thought in these past few weeks that perhaps it is time for the Master of Sinanju to retire his sword. To let a younger, better man take his place."

Remo started to speak, but Chiun silenced him with a pointed finger.

"I have thought of who would replace me. Who would labor so that my village would be supported? So that the poor of Sinanju would be fed and clothed and housed? I could think of no Korean who could do it, who would do it. I could think only of you."

"It is a great honor you pay me," Remo said, "just in speaking the words."

"Silence," Chiun commanded. "You are, after all, almost a Korean. If

27

you could learn to control your appetite and your mouth, you would be a fine master."

"My pride knows no bounds," Remo said.

"So I have thought of this for many weeks. And I have told myself: Chiun, you are getting too old. There have been too many years and too many battles. Already, Remo is your equal. Silence! I have said, already Remo is your equal. And I have felt my strength waning as I thought these things, and I have said, no one needs Chiun any longer, no one needs him to be the Master of Sinanju, he is old and his meager talents have vanished, and whatever he can do, Remo can do better. I have told myself all these things." His voice was sonorous and deep, now, as if delivering a sermon he had spent years mastering. What was he leading up to? Remo wondered.

"Yes," Chiun said, "I have thought all these things." Remo saw his eyes twinkle. He was enjoying it, the whole speech. The old fraud.

"And now I have reached my decision."

"I am sure it is wise and just," Remo said, cautiously, not trusting the old fox.

"The decision was forced upon me when you dispatched that baboon with your elbow."

"Yes?" Remo said, slowly.

"Do you realize your fist was a full eight inches away from your chest when you struck?"

"I did not know that, little father."

"No, of course, you did not. And in that instant, wisdom came to me."

"Yes?"

"Wisdom came to me," Chiun said, "and it said, how can you turn the welfare of Sinanju over to a man who does not even know to keep his fist against his chest when performing the back elbow thrust? I ask your answer to that question, Remo."

"In conscience, you could not entrust Sinanju to such a worthless one as me."

"That is true," Chiun said. "Watching your inept performance, suddenly I realized that Chiun was not so old and worthless after all. That it would be many years before you are ready to replace him."

"You speak only truth," Remo said.

"So we must resume our training to prepare you for that day. When it comes. Five or six years from now."

Chiun swirled onto his feet. "We must practice the back elbow thrust. You perform it as a child. You disgrace my training and my name. Your lack of talent is an insult to my ancestors. Your clumsiness is an insult to me."

Chiun was working himself up into a lather. Remo, who an hour before had despaired over Chiun's will to live, now realized how insufferable and overbearing he would be. An hour ago, he would have been overjoyed if Chiun would accompany him on his next job; now, he would make sure not to invite him.

Remo stood. "You are right, Chiun, that I need the training. But it must wait. I have an assignment."

"You will need my assistance. One who cannot even keep his fist next to his chest cannot be expected to perform creditably."

"No, Chiun," Remo said. "This is a very easy assignment. I will be done with it and returned before you even have time to pack. Then we will go on vacation."

"And then we will practice the back elbow thrust," Chiun corrected.

"That too," Remo said.

Chiun said nothing. But he looked pleased.

CHAPTER FIVE

BARON ISAAC NEMEROFF HAD RENTED the entire penthouse floor of the Stonewall Hotel in Algiers.

He had done it in a manner unusual for the man who owned the corporation that owned the corporation that owned the hotel. He had sent a telegram to the hotel management asking to lease the floor for six months.

He had sent telegrams to decorators and builders advising them that he wanted special remodeling work done on the penthouse floor.

He had sent a telegram to the telephone company requesting that a company representative discuss with one of his aides the phone service required to be installed, including special conference lines and scrambler devices.

By telegram, he had hired sound experts from Rome to make sure that the central section of the penthouse, which had been remodeled into a conference room, was absolutely unbugged.

It had taken him three weeks to do all these things and at the end of the third week, a small news item appeared in the Algiers English-language paper:

What's on tap for the fabulously wealthy Baron Isaac Nemeroff? He's taken over the entire penthouse floor of the Stonewall Hotel, remodeled it and installed security devices that would do credit to the American Secret Service. Must be something big in the wind for the Baron. Hmmmm?

Baron Nemeroff saw the news item while eating his daily breakfast, which unfailingly consisted of orange juice, grape juice, four eggs, one chocolate éclair, and coffee with milk and four spoonfuls of sugar.

He sat on one of the patios of his gargantuan estate, high on a hill overlooking the interior city of Algiers, nodding his head in approval of the story. He folded the paper and placed it carefully on the table next to his empty juice glasses. He wiped his mouth and swallowed the last few flakes of éclair which he scooped up off the cake plate with his fingertips.

Only then did he laugh.

The baron's laugh was not a pleasant event. It sounded like a bray, and looked as if it should have been a bray, because it came from a face that was mule-like. Nemeroff's head was long and rectangular, with a jutting jaw and a sloped forehead. A thick shock of red hair flew backwards from the top of his skull. His eyes were big and seemed to be vertical ovals. The long, broad triangle of his nose was pasted grossly on a face whose skin was pale, freckled and testified to the anguish of sunburn.

Nemeroff was six-feet-eight inches tall, weighed 156 pounds, and he required six meals a day to keep his weight that high. A metabolic imbalance burned up energy as fast as he could take it in. His body was always moving; a foot shook as it dangled over his other leg, his hands drummed on the table, he waved as if to shoo off imaginary insects. His sleep was restless, troubled and twitchy, and could cost him five pounds of his weight.

Missing a meal or two could drop his weight ten pounds. He would starve to death within seventy-two hours.

So he stuffed himself like a caged goose being readied for liver pate.

And now he laughed; it was an evil, hectic laugh that shook his body and seemed visibly to burn up some of his store of energy.

He looked from his balcony toward the central city of Algiers, lying low before him, crowned by its tallest building, the Stonewall Hotel, and he laughed some more.

It had gone exactly as he had planned. The intelligence experts of nations around the world would spend their time breaking into, bugging, de-bugging, bugging each other's bugs, tripping over each other, trying to find out what was happening on the 35th floor of the Stonewall Hotel.

He brayed some more. They should have asked; he could have told them. Absolutely nothing was happening there.

The whole thing had been a front, a ruse to keep intruders away from his estate, where the Baron's real business would be conducted during the next several days.

He left nothing to chance.

And now, the moment of hilarity over, he looked at his breakfast guest, the sweating hulk of jelly who would soon be the president of Scambia.

Vice President Asiphar had been watching the baron intently, wanting to inquire into the cause of his good humor, but afraid it would be unseemly.

"It all goes well, my vice president," Nemeroff said. His voice was reedy and high-pitched. "Forgive my laughing, but I was thinking of how foolish are the men who would stop us, and how cleverly we will outwit them, you and I."

"And your guests?" asked Asiphar, who pushed away from in front of him the remnants of a Ry-Krisp cracker, which, along with black coffee, had been his breakfast.

"They will begin arriving in the next day. Come, let me show you our arrangements."

He stood quickly, and did not notice the look of disappointment on Asiphar's face. The vice president followed him to the edge of the balcony and turned his face in the direction of the baron's outstretched hand.

"You'll notice that there is only one road leading to this villa," he said. "And, of course, there are armed guards along its length. Every visitor must be approved by me. There is no other way for a car to approach."

Down came the arm, quickly, and up went the other, sweeping back and forth across the vegetation-shrouded hill that sloped away from them.

"There are men stationed all over those slopes," Nemeroff said. "Armed men, who will know how to handle any would-be intruders.

And dogs, whose appetite for unwanted company leaves nothing to be desired." He brayed once, softly. "And there are electronic devices, electric eyes, infrared television cameras, hidden microphones, that can detect and pinpoint the presence of any intruder immediately."

He turned away from the balcony. He shot both hands skyward, over his head. "And, of course, our helicopter fleet continually patrols the sky over the castle." Asiphar looked upward. One plane circled lazily over the stone pile that was Nemeroff's castle, its silhouette a deep red — almost black — against the washed-out blue sky.

Nemeroff turned from the rail and put his arm over the shoulder and around the massive back of Asiphar.

"So it is foolproof, my vice president. We shall not be disturbed."

Gently, he steered Asiphar toward the glass doors that led into the castle. "Come, I will show you our meeting facilities, and you must tell me of your flight from Switzerland. How were the stewardesses?"

He brayed and listened intently as Asiphar described the women on the plane. In great detail.

Nemeroff was dressed in white, from neck to toe and the white seemed more brilliant than the fine linen it was, against the backdrop of Asiphar's dark suit. The vice president had travelled incognito from Switzerland, and so had stored his uniforms away, wearing only a black silk suit. It was soaked through now with perspiration and under the arms were white granular rings where his sweat had saturated the suit, and then dried, leaving only the salt remains.

The two men stood in front of an immense oil painting of a Russian Cossack, in battle array, atop a black charger as Nemeroff explained "There are seventy rooms in the castle, more than enough for all our... business associates." He pressed a button, hidden in the wooden frame of the painting, and the painting silently slid aside, revealing a small stainless steel elevator compartment.

They stepped inside and Nemeroff pressed a button marked V.

Noiselessly, without even the sensation of starting, the elevator moved upward. Quickly, the door opened, and they stepped out into a giant room, fully one hundred feet long and forty feet wide. Its walls were hewn of the same rough stone of which the castle itself had been built.

The room was so large it dwarfed the giant mahogany conference table that had been set up in its direct center, but as Asiphar looked, he slowly realized that the table held chairs for forty men. The chairs were of soft red glove leather, and in front of each chair on the table was a desk blotter, a yellow pad, a silver tray of pencils, a carafe, and a crystal stem goblet.

"Our meetings will be held here," Nemeroff said. "In this very room, within the next three days, will be made the decisions that will make you president of your nation."

Asiphar smiled, his white teeth playing lighthouse in the night of his face.

"...and will make your nation a power among the powers of the earth," Nemeroff said, his arms gesticulating wildly.

"Imagine," he said, slowly walking Asiphar around the room. "A nation that is under crime's flag. A retreat for all the hunted of the world. The place where no power can touch them. And you will control that nation. You, Asiphar. You will be a man among men. The most powerful man in the world."

He smiled, a grim, thin-lipped smile that spoke more truth than his words, but Asiphar did not see his smile.

His eyes, instead, were drawn to an immense dome in the center of the room's ceiling, through which sunlight poured into the conference room. The dome was of stained glass, in carefully leaded sections worked into a symbolic Byzantine religious design.

Nemeroff followed his eyes. "It is quite bulletproof," he said. "And beautiful, is it not? And up there are our helicopter pads."

"And your guests will arrive tomorrow?" Asiphar asked, unable to keep the anxiety from his voice.

And Nemeroff understood. "Our business guests," he said. "There are other house guests here now. One in particular whom you must meet. Come, I will introduce you. You must be tired after your journey, and I can think of no more certain way for you to relax."

Asiphar giggled.

They reentered the elevator and Nemeroff pressed the button marked IV. The door closed, then reopened again before Asiphar had felt any sense of movement.

They stepped out into a long, wide hallway, carpeted with animal skins, its walls mirrored in a delicate gold-veined pattern. Along the walls stood marble statuary depicting naked bodies. The carvings showed the great skill and even genius of the craftsmen, and the stone blocks themselves showed the precise taste of Nemeroff. The marble blocks, from which the statues had been carved by his order, were pure white, recrystallized limestone, with none of the pinkness that confessed to manganese oxide traces. The stones had come from a quarry Nemeroff owned, in the hills of northern Italy.

He ignored the statues, steering Asiphar down the hall to the right. "This way," he said.

He paused at an unnumbered door, not distinguished from the other doors all along the hallway. He knocked once, softly, then pushed open the door. It swung open noiselessly, and he stepped aside to let Asiphar peer in.

It was a bedroom, its walls and floor covered with red woolen carpet and its ceiling mirrored, in glass blocks with streaks of gold and black swirling through them.

The bed was a huge four-poster, with a red fringe around the posts, but there was no canopy over the top, permitting an unobstructed view of the mirrored ceiling.

On the bed lay a woman. She was tall-looking, even in repose, and her skin was so fair that it appeared never to have seen a day's sun. She wore a long white transparent negligee that hid her skin only when the sheer material was formed into a fold. The negligee was open. Her long almost-white hair, was pulled in front of a shoulder and casually covered one breast. The other breast was bare, and full and crowned with a delicate pink mound. She was blonde all over.

She stood up and walked slowly toward the door, not caring that her negligee was fully open and trailing behind her. Her eyes lighted with excitement and her mouth partially open, revealing perfectly even lines of teeth, she extended her arms toward Asiphar.

"As you see, she has been awaiting you," Nemeroff said.

Asiphar could not speak. Then, his throat dry and sandy, he crackled, "Thank you."

"She is lovely, is she not?" Nemeroff said. The girl stood in front of them now — lush, inviting — her arms still extended toward Asiphar.

"Look at those breasts," Nemeroff said. "Those legs. Do you agree she could make a man forget the cares of burdensome office?"

Again, dry-throated, Asiphar croaked, "Yes."

"She is yours. She waits only to serve you. To do for you anything you wish."

"Anything?"

"Anything," Nemeroff said coldly. "And if she does not please you, there are others who will." He looked at the woman now, meeting her eyes for the first time. More perceptive eyes than Asiphar's might have noticed the glimmer of fear which crossed her face, disappearing almost immediately, and the grimace of scorn and hatred on Nemeroff's face.

But Asiphar noted nothing, only the breasts, inviting him, and the hips and legs, inviting him, and the opened arms, calling for him. His breath came harder, and Nemeroff finally said, "I will leave you two to get acquainted. You must lunch with me, my friend. On the terrace at one."

Then he gently pushed Asiphar into the room and closed the door behind the two.

Quickly, Nemeroff walked back to the elevator and pushed the button marked III.

The elevator opened again into a hallway, identical with the one Nemeroff had just left, except that there was only one door in sight.

That door led to the suite of rooms which were Nemeroff's own living quarters, and he went through it now, through a living room, through a bedroom, and into a large, bare study in the corner of the building.

He locked the door behind him, went to a large wall cabinet, and pulled open its doors.

The cabinet held a 46-inch television screen, with a panel of buttons and controls on its right side. Nemeroff turned one dial to 4 and another one to A, then pressed a button.

He sat down in a contoured foam chair, which reclined under his weight. The television screen lightened, flashed into blue color at the side, and then a picture came into view.

It was Asiphar lying naked in the bed, alongside the woman, his blue-black skin accenting the smooth whiteness of her body. His hand was around her shoulder. Her left hand went out to Asiphar's body. Her right hand reached down to pick up something off the floor. It came back into view carrying a small, battery-operated vibrator.

Nemeroff felt a tremor of excitement. He leaned forward and pressed a button marked "tape," then sank back softly in the chair to watch his favorite television show.

CHAPTER SIX

REMO SANK BACK IN THE soft, cushioned seat of the big jetliner. When John F. Kennedy International Airport receded in the distance, back beyond the left wing, Remo kicked off his loafers, stretched his legs, took a magazine from the wall rack next to his seat, and, over the top of the magazine, eyed the stewardesses.

He had never understood why men went for stewardesses. They represented the ultimate triumph of plastic in a world of flesh and blood. There was only one step to go past the dehumanization they represented: the robot. And when one was invented and it looked real enough, the first buyer would be the airlines who would paste on a pair of 34C's, a thirty-two-tooth smile, and turn them loose down the aisles of their planes.

"I'm XB-27, fly me. I'm XB-27, fly me. I'm XB-27, fly me."

Remo watched as one blonde stew lectured a passenger in an aisle seat three rows in front of Remo. The passenger had a cigarette burning; the no-smoking sign was still on.

Remo turned up his hearing to listen in.

"I'm sorry, sir, you'll have to put out that cigarette."

"I'm not going to set anything on fire," the man replied. He waved the cigarette at the girl. He held it with his thumb on one side, his index and middle fingers on the other, and he used its lit end as a pointer when he talked. The gesture struck Remo as familiar.

"I'm sorry, sir, but you must obey the rules, or I'll have to call the pilot." She was still smiling.

"I'll tell you what," the man answered. "You call the pilot. You call the whole goddam air force if you want. I'm smoking this cigarette." That voice. It raised a stirring somewhere in Remo's memory. He tried to place it.

He leaned forward in his seat for a better view of the man's profile.

No help there.

He was a medium-tall man, lean, with a baby face and horn-rimmed glasses; Remo had never seen the face before. Then the man turned slightly in his seat, gave Remo a little more than a quarter view, and Remo noticed something else: the slight puff of scar tissue around the eyes, and as the man kept turning, Remo saw the same artificially-taut skin around the nose.

Remo recognized it. He had seen it often enough on his own face. The residue of the plastic surgeon's craft. Whoever he was, the man with the cigarette had had his face changed.

He was still jawing with the stewardess. Remo remembered what made his voice familiar. It was guttural New Jersey, the accent Remo had been brought up with until CURE had throatwashed him of it and retrained his speech in the bland middle-American pattern that admitted no antecedents.

The man jabbed the point of the cigarette toward the stewardess again. Where had Remo seen that gesture before?

The scene lost its potential for ugliness, all at once, when the no-smoking light flashed off.

"There," the man said, his voice harsh and wrong sounding, coming out of that gentle, delicate-featured face. "See. It's all right now."

The stewardess turned around, glanced at the sign, smiled wanly and walked away. The man in the seat followed every movement with his eyes. She disappeared into the cabin up front and the man relaxed, then looked around, over both shoulders, and Remo conscientiously looked out the window, watching the man's reflection in the glass.

Finally, the man stabbed out the cigarette with a thrust that left it half-burning in the seat-arm ashtray, stood up and walked toward the lounge in the rear of the plane. Remo wondered if the psychology of entertainment on an airliner was sound. Didn't people wonder if you were spending too much time booking acts and too little time overhauling jet engines? Remo did.

He returned to his magazine, trying to concentrate, but the voice and the gestures with the cigarette kept intruding on his mind. Where? When? A few minutes later, the blonde stewardess appeared again in the aisle, walking toward the rear of the plane.

Remo beckoned to her.

"Yes sir," she said, leaning over him, smiling.

Remo smiled back. "That loudmouth. With the cigarette before. What's his name?"

She started to protest, to protect the good name of her passengers, and then Remo's smile made her think better of it.

"Oh, that's Mr. Johnson," she said.

"Johnson? He have a first name?"

She looked at the clipboard in her hands.

"As a matter of fact, he doesn't," she said. "Just initials. P.K. Johnson."

"Oh," Remo said. "Too bad. I thought he was someone I knew. Thank you."

"You're welcome, sir." She kept leaning forward, close now to the man with the wonderful smile. "Is there anything I can do? Anything at all to make you comfortable?"

"Yes. Join me in prayer that the wings don't fall off."

She stood straight up, not sure if he was joking or not, but he smiled again, deliciously warm, she thought, and she walked away contentedly. Remo sat back deep into the cushion.

P.K. Johnson. It meant nothing. Now what had CURE taught him? When people adopted fake names, they generally kept their own initials? All right. P.K.J. John P. something. P.K. Remo detested intellectual exercise. P.J.K.

P.J.! P.J. Kenny.

Of course. He had seen that cigarette-holding number once before, when he was arresting P.J. Kenny on a gambling charge.

Remo had been a rookie patrolman, walking a beat in the Ironbound section of Newark. He was walking past the storefront headquarters of somebody's Social and Athletic Club — the kind that proliferated every mayoral election year — and when he glanced inside the brightly lighted room, he saw men, sitting at a table, playing cards, with mounds of bills and silver stacked on the table.

Gambling was against the law in New Jersey, even though no one seemed to notice. Remo did what he thought was best.

He stepped inside the clubrooms, and waited until he was noticed.

"Sorry, fellas," he said with a smile, "you'll have to close down the game. Or move to a back room where people can't see you from the street."

There were six players at the table. All had large stacks of money in front of them, except one. He was a tall, lean man; his nose was squashed over his face and he had scars over both eyes. He had only a few singles on the table in front of him.

The others at the table turned to look at him. He carefully inspected his cards, then looked up at Remo, slowly, contemptuously.

"Fuck off, kid," he said. There was no humor in his voice. It was thick, guttural, New Jersey street talk.

Remo decided to ignore it. "You'll have to end the game, men," he said again.

"And I said, fuck off."

"You've got a big mouth, mister," Remo said.

"I got more than that," the man said. He stood up, pulled his cigarette from the ashtray, and came toward Remo.

He stood in front of him and said again, "Fuck off."

"You're under arrest."

"Yeah? What's the charge?"

"Gambling. And interfering with an officer."

"Sonny, do you know who I am?"

"No," Remo said, "and I don't care."

"My name's Kenny. And in forty-eight hours, I'm going to have you dragging ass on some miserable beat in Niggertown."

"You do that," Remo said. "But do it from jail. You're under arrest."

Then the cigarette pointed toward his face, held that way between thumb, index and middle fingers, and it punctuated Kenny's words.

"You're going to be sorry."

He booked Kenny that night for gambling and interfering with an officer. Forty-eight hours later, Remo was walking a beat in the heart of the black ghetto. P.J. Kenny's attorney waived a hearing in municipal

41

court and the case was sent to the grand jury. It was never heard of again.

Remo never forgot the incident. It was one of the first of a series of disappointments he encountered, when he tried to act as if the law were on the level.

From his beat in the ghetto, Remo was framed for murder and brought to work for CURE, after having been "executed" in the state prison in an electric chair that didn't work.

P.J. Kenny moved on to better things, too.

He became well-known in gangland as a professional killer who hired out to all sides. He was the top contract man, the man who never missed.

He had a reputation a department store would envy. He was all business and he gave top value for the dollar.

Because he was so good, he was feared, and thus he never became a target for one side or the other in the gang wars that periodically infected the country.

It was known that there was no animosity in his work, no personal enmity. He was just a professional. And a side that knew it had lost a man to P.J. Kenny seemed not to take it personally. If they came up with the right price, they could hire him themselves to even the score.

He turned down dozens of offers to join forces with different families. He was probably wise, because it was his reputation for even-handedness that kept him alive. He was not a partisan and therefore not a man partisans should go after.

One man had tried it once, after P.J. had carried off a contract against the son of a mob leader. The hood was trying to impress his boss. The hood wound up dead, along with his father, two brothers, wife and daughter. All carved with a knife like Thanksgiving turkeys.

That was the last time anyone took personal umbrage at any contract P.J. Kenny carried out. Now he was considered the Tiffany of the trade, and he had more work than he could handle.

Then a few months ago, there had been a Senate investigation into racketeering. A subpoena was issued for P.J. Kenny to testify. He vanished. Remo had read it in the papers and hoped that CURE would be involved, that he would have a chance to go after P.J. Kenny.

But CURE wasn't, he didn't, the Senate hearing died out, and P.J. Kenny remained out of sight.

And now here he was, with a new face, on his way to Algeria. Smith's report had told Remo that many of the top Mafia leaders in the country were on their way to meet with Baron Nemeroff.

Was there any doubt that P.J. Kenny was traveling on a professional mission? Nobody vacationed in Algeria. Not even Algerians.

Remo read, while the plane whistled on across the Atlantic, double-timing from day to night.

Remo heard steps behind him and glanced up as Kenny walked down the aisle of the plane, swaying from side to side, drunk from seven straight hours at the bar in the lounge.

He staggered to his seat, sat down heavily and looked around belligerently. His eyes caught Remo's and he tried to stare Remo down. He finally gave up, turned around and slumped back into his seat.

The blonde stewardess came from the pilot's cabin and walked slowly down the aisle, her head clicking from side to side, looking to see if passengers needed anything.

Remo heard P.J.'s guttural voice. "Come here, girl."

From his seat, Remo saw the young blonde step up to Kenny. "Is there something I can do for you?" she said, smiling, willing to let bygones be bygones, as they learned in lesson seven at stewardess school.

"Yeah," Kenny growled. He motioned for the girl to come closer and he spoke softly in her ear. Remo saw her face turn red with embarrassment, and then, just as suddenly, turn into a pain-filled mask.

P.J. had his hand up under her skirt and Remo could tell he was squeezing her flesh. It must have hurt too much for her to yell.

P.J. laughed and put his other hand on her wrist, then pulled her down toward him again. Her face was still pained, and his left hand was still working under her skirt. He spoke again into her ear, cruelly, viciously, and Remo could see tears welling in her eyes.

He got up from his seat and walked forward to the aisle seat where P.J. Kenny held the girl prisoner in his grip.

"Johnson," he said.

There was a pause, then Kenny looked over his shoulder at Remo.

"Yeah. What do you want?"

"Let go of the girl. We've got to talk."

"I don't want to talk," he said thickly. "I don't want to let go of the girl."

Remo leaned close to Kenny's face. "Let go of that girl or I'll peel that scar tissue off your face and stuff it down your throat."

Kenny looked up again — annoyed this time, as well as surprised. He hesitated a moment and released the girl.

Remo took her hands in his. "I'm sorry, Miss." Tears streamed down her face. "Mr. Johnson had too much to drink. It won't happen again."

"Hey there," Kenny demanded. "Whaddya mean, too much to drink?"

"Just close your face," Remo said. He released the girl's hands with a comforting squeeze, then watched as she slowly walked away, up the aisle.

Remo slid past Kenny's knees and took the seat next to him.

"Your face looks pretty good," he said.

"Yeah?" Kenny answered suspiciously. "Yours doesn't."

"I'll have to get the address of your plastic surgeon. Maybe he can make me as distinguished looking as you."

"Look, mister," Kenny said. "I don't know who you are or what you want, but why don't you just fuck off?"

"I'm from Nemeroff," Remo said.

"Yeah? Who's Nemeroff?"

"Don't get cute with me," Remo said. "You know damn well who he is. He's the guy you're taking this trip for."

"Pal," Kenny snorted. "I don't know you and I don't like you. Already, I could find a reason to do some things to you that ain't pleasant. Now get lost."

"I'd love to. Except I'm your contact man. I'm supposed to get you to Nemeroff. In one piece. That means without being beaten up by some airline stewardess or arrested by airport police for having a phony passport."

"What's your name?" Kenny asked.

"Roger Willis."

"I never heard of you," Kenny said.

"I've heard of you, Mr. Kenny. So has the baron. That's why he sent me. To keep you out of trouble."

"You got any identification?" Kenny asked.

"In my briefcase."

"Get it," Kenny said.

Remo looked around him, then up at the overhead oxygen mask. It would be pleasant to give Kenny a demonstration of how it worked and cut off the air supply. Too risky. Too much chance of people wandering by.

"You've really slipped," Remo said. "Sure, I'll open my briefcase out here, so that every nosy bastard on the plane can come by and snoop into our business. The lavatory. Five minutes. The one on the left, leave the lock open."

He got up without waiting for an answer, stepped over Kenny's legs and returned to his own seat.

Remo glanced at his watch. The plane should be nearing its destination in a few minutes. He wanted to shave the time just right.

Five minutes later, Kenny got up and walked toward the center of the plane. Remo nodded to him as he passed. He waited a minute, then stood up and followed.

Kenny was washing his face at the sink when Remo entered the little cubicle and his eyes met Remo's in the mirror. There was a glint of metal at Kenny's wrist and Remo remembered he carried a knife in his sleeve.

Kenny patted his face delicately with a towel from a pile over the sink, put back on his eyeglasses, and turned to Remo.

"Now where's your identification?" he said.

"Right here," Remo said. His left hand flicked out and the fingernails raked the skin over Kenny's left eye, tearing up the tissue-paper thin scar tissue, and sending blood streaming down Kenny's face. "That identifies me as a guy who doesn't like to see women beaten up."

"Bastard," Kenny growled. He flicked his arm toward the floor, hard; the handle of the knife was in his hand, and then it was pointed at Remo's midsection. "When I'm done with you, they'll identify you by my initials on the inside of your stomach."

"You're forgetting Nemeroff. I'm his man," Remo said.

"Screw Nemeroff. He hired me to be around if he needs me. He didn't hire me to be pushed around by some punk."

Remo backed off, with only inches separating him from Kenny.

45

"Is this any way to greet an old friend?" Remo asked.

"Old friend, huh?" Kenny glowered.

"Sure. We met in Newark. Oh, maybe ten years ago. Don't you remember?"

Kenny was wavering. "No."

"Yeah. I arrested you for gambling. You had me transferred off my beat."

Kenny's eyes squinted behind the glasses, trying to remember. He did. "You're a cop," he hissed. "A goddam cop. No wonder."

"Take a good look, you pail of garbage. It's the last face you'll ever see," Remo said.

Kenny lunged with the knife and Remo slid alongside the thrust. The blade hit the metal door and the force of the stroke skidded the blade along the door, until it slipped into the crack between the door and the frame. Remo slapped the door open, and the movement snapped off the knife blade, and then the edge of Remo's hand hit Kenny in the face.

He jolted backward, onto the toilet seat, dropping the knife-handle. Then Remo was on him, an arm under Kenny's arm, the heel of his hand against the back of Kenny's neck, pressing it forward, cutting off the air. He forced Kenny over the shallow sink and shoved his head down into it. He ran the water until the sink was full, and he kept Kenny's face down under the water. In the confines of the tiny room there was little opportunity to move about or gain leverage. Remo was on him like a vise. First there was bubbling and then thrashing, then just silent limpness.

Already, his trip was a success, Remo thought. P.J. Kenny. Good. And that could be his passport to Nemeroff. Passport.

He reached into Kenny's jacket pocket and took his billfold and passport. Still holding Kenny in the sink, he flipped open the passport. It was made out in the name of Johnson and carried the picture of the new Kenny — horn-rimmed, country-doctor glasses and all. Remo took his passport from his hip pocket and slid it into Kenny's jacket. The dead man was now Roger Willis.

So much for that.

He dried Kenny's face and hair with a towel, then arranged him on the toilet seat. Kenny's body slumped against the wall. His glasses hung from only one earpiece.

The glasses. Remo took them. He'd need them, if they checked passports. The horn rims would fool anyone, particularly passport checkers to whom all faces looked alike anyway.

He started to leave, and remembered Kenny's face. Even with the passport for Roger Willis, someone might recognize him as Kenny. Probably that blonde stewardess.

With his fingernails he made sure no one would ever recognize Kenny again.

He then washed his hands and slipped Kenny's eyeglasses in his shirt pocket.

Stepping out of the lavatory, he smashed the side of his hand twice against the hinges of the door, crushing the metal, making sure it would not open to a casual push.

He would be long gone, before they found P.J. Kenny's body.

Before anyone was ever able to identify the corpse as P.J. Kenny's, Remo would be done with Baron Nemeroff and Vice President Asiphar. It should all work very well.

Remo walked back down the aisle, and with no stewardess in sight, took the attaché case from under Kenny's seat.

He got back into his own seat just as the "fasten safety belts" light came on.

The blonde walked up the aisle, checking seat belts. She smiled at Remo and he smiled back.

He wondered what her expression would be after they'd landed, and they found the body sitting on the john. Or later, when they determined that he had died of drowning.

Probably, she'd smile.

Remo would.

CHAPTER SEVEN

Baron isaac nemeroff had sent telegrams of summons all over the world, and all over the world men prepared to come.

From the top families of the American Mafia to the leading producer and purveyor of pornography in the world — a Japanese who owned and operated brothels and film processing plants in more than fifteen countries — they prepared to come. Men who controlled thousands of acres of land, now turned over to the growing of poppies, made ready to come. From the bowels of crime would come the professional gamblers who owned those casinos around the world which once had been expected to drive criminals out of gambling. From Switzerland would come a seventy-two-year-old man whose name was probably unknown to everyone but Nemeroff, who knew him as the greatest counterfeiter in the world, a man who had printed literally billions of dollars of queer and floated it into the world money-markets from his Swiss headquarters.

There would be smugglers, gun-runners, swindlers, the head of a ring of jewel thieves.

When Nemeroff called, they would all come.

And most of them were not sure of why. Few had ever met him, which was as Nemeroff wanted it, since he was not a public man. His name did not make gossip columns unless he wished it to. He did not allow himself to be thought of as phony Russian nobility, another fraud who declared himself baron three days after learning which fork to use.

His credentials as nobility were impeccable. He chose to live his life to meet the arbitrary standards he had set for that nobility.

Nemeroff was forty-six years old, the only son of a beautiful young Frenchwoman, and a Russian father whose ancestry was connected with the Romanoffs and whose capacity for anger was connected with the Cossacks.

Young Isaac had been born in Paris, and soon after his birth, his mother died under circumstances that could only be described as suspicious.

Those who knew the old Count Nemeroff knew that there was nothing suspicious about it. His wife was a trollop, of noble birth, but a trollop nonetheless, and upon finding himself cuckolded, Nemeroff had simply poisoned her.

There was almost no Nemeroff fortune left, the Russian revolution having taken care of that. But his mother left young Isaac and his father a comfortable amount of money, which his father found decidedly uncomfortable.

The old man and the boy then began to live the life of wanderers, traveling continuously from year to year, from one pleasure capital of the world to the next. And everywhere there were beautiful women for Count Nemeroff, to provide him with the funds to at least imitate his former life style.

Young Isaac grew to hate them, with their brittle faces and alabaster skins, and their staged, identical, musical laughs. He hated them as rivals for his father's affection. He hated them most when he saw them slip envelopes into his father's pockets and he hated the look on his father's face when he opened the envelope and counted the cash it contained, when in their carriage on the way back to their hotel.

Isaac was eight years old when he became a thief. He had already been well-grounded in the important currencies of the world: diamonds were best, gold next, other precious metals, stones and American dollars following somewhat after that.

He specialized in diamonds.

While he was supposed to be at poolside at some rich woman's villa and his father was inside tending to her needs; when he could hear the laughter and the sighs floating softly through a window; he would leave the pool and wander the house. A pin here. A ring, there. A brooch. He avoided necklaces because he thought their absence would be too quickly noted. He gave no thought as to what he would do with his booty. He carried the pieces in a shaving kit which he kept in his suitcase, and which his father never opened, thinking its possession merely a young boy's affectation.

When he was a few years older, he rented a safe-deposit box in a Swiss bank and began keeping his jewelry there. Upon each of their subsequent trips to Switzerland, he would take out one of the pieces, break the jewels from their mountings and sell them to a diamond dealer.

Isaac, though only twelve, was already over six feet tall, and seemed to grow so rapidly that his clothes were always ill-fitting. He was conscious of his wrists extending from his sleeves and his ankles visible below his cuffs when he went to see the first diamond merchant on the list of names he had copied from a telephone book.

The merchant, a kindly-appearing old man with a walrus mustache, had looked at Isaac, at his long, sad face, at his ill-fitting clothes and had laughed aloud and put Isaac out of his office. Years later, Isaac bought the firm, hired accountants for the sole purpose of finding errors in the books, and through criminal and civil actions in the courts hounded the former owner into suicide.

But he had to go no farther than the second name on his list to find a merchant who would buy his stones. He was paid $10,000 American dollars, one-tenth of what the flawless diamonds were worth. He was happy to get it. The cash went into a numbered bank account.

By the time he was fourteen, he had stolen more than a million dollars in jewelry, and had more than one hundred thousand American dollars in his account.

His father was still penniless, still trading his genitalia for meals, still apologetic to Isaac that he could not provide him with all the things a young boy should have in life. Isaac only smiled.

Then came the Second World War and suddenly his father's fortunes improved.

While he had no money of his own, his life had been spent with the international moneyed set and in a war of shifting alliances and backroom power plays, access to the moneyed class was important, important enough for Count Nemeroff to become a sought-after man.

He became a messenger, a negotiator, a promoter for all sides.

He ran guns to Spain, inventing the technique of selling the same shipment to both sides, then leaving the shipment in the middle of the field equidistant from both camps, letting the two sides fight for them. He sold information to the British; he arranged for opium to be gotten into Europe from China; he dealt with the American Mafia to make inroads into Italy's government.

And in 1943, he died of a massive cerebral hemorrhage.

Governments on both sides mourned; they were truly grieved. He was indispensable; was able to do for governments the things government could do not for themselves. How could he be replaced?

They had not counted on young Isaac, however. He had been a good student. He kept track of the names and the power and the predilections of the people with whom his father had dealt and at his father's graveside, even as the old count was being shoveled into earth, he let it be known that the Nemeroff family would still be doing business at the same old stand, in the person of the fourteenth Baron Nemeroff.

They scoffed at first; he was too young. But as their problems mounted and grew more complex, at last — in desperation — they turned to Isaac. And he delivered, even better than his father had done.

But where his father had been content to work for cash, for money on the barrelhead, Isaac was not. He already had money; he sought power — power to do things, to build things.

From France, in return for a favor, he demanded a controlling portion of a chemical factory, whose operation was critical to the late war effort and for which he had managed to make available the raw materials.

From Germany, he accepted part ownership of a munitions factory, and so widespread was his influence that when Germany lost the war, his claim to ownership was not disputed by the allies.

His empire spread. At nineteen, he was not only a millionaire many times over, but a conglomerate — controlling scores of businesses and with influence in scores more.

He had selected those businesses with care. The chemical factory in

France would one day handle the processing of heroin; the German munitions factory would provide guns for guerrilla wars, and non-traceable weapons for those willing to pay the price.

He was driven by a lust never to be poor again, and, beyond that, to have power. Power that no stroke of bad luck — no matter how long, no matter how deadly — could diminish. He would never be in the position of groveling as his father had groveled before those painted women whose money was able to cover their shallowness and stupidity. This Baron Isaac Nemeroff would never accept an envelope.

He never had to. And when peace came and governments no longer had need of his power and influence, he looked for a new field of endeavor to replace war. He selected crime.

He would never steal again; he was beyond that. But he would become an ombudsman for international crime. If there was a problem to be solved, he would solve it.

If weaponry were needed, he could produce it. If political influence were required, he could exert it. If judges had to be made to see the light of sweet reason, he could give them very good and ample reasons to do so. When drug shipments were bogged down because of periodic governmental crackdowns, Nemeroff could move them.

He was not in crime, but he was of crime. He refused to accept the label of criminal. He told himself he was a management analyst, providing a service to the highest bidder. And while it was unlikely, he told himself he would have done the same job for any legally-established government which had retained him.

He rarely dealt with any criminal leader directly. But it seemed that most problems of and for crime had a way of ending up on the desk of some obscure company in this city or that. And behind the desk, a bright-eyed young man would promise to "look into it," and within only a few hours, he would report back to his client that "Baron Nemeroff said that you may have it," or "Baron Nemeroff said to do it for you as a favor." Heroin would move, guns would be produced, judges would be bribed and crime would move on as smoothly as before.

The brighter ones might ask the bright-eyed young men, "Just who is this Baron Nemeroff?" And the young men would smile and invariably answer: "The man who can straighten things out for you."

One of the things that he had been called on to straighten out was a hiding place for an American criminal, fleeing prosecution. He had done it. And then, within a period of two months, three more major criminals had asked him to find them sanctuary. He had.

The western world was in the middle of one of its periodic crackdowns on crime. It occurred to Nemeroff that the solution to the problem of asylum for criminals might be one for his brain to explore.

Then, one night, he had met Vice President Asiphar in a London gambling casino, and all the pieces suddenly fell into place.

The casino arranged for Asiphar to lose, far beyond his means, and Nemeroff had stepped forward to arrange payment of the sweating hulk's debts. That had brought Asiphar into his orbit. He was kept there at the moment with occasional funds and frequent women, always women of the whitest possible skin.

But Nemeroff distrusted the power of women to permanently lock Asiphar to him. The television tapings of the vice president's bed sessions were a precaution, against any inclination by Asiphar to reconsider.

It had taken Nemeroff six months to work out the plan, and another three to win Asiphar fully to his side. The scheme was simple:

Assassinate President Dashiti, install Asiphar as president, and put Scambia under crime's flag.

It was now all ready to go and Nemeroff had sent out 40 telegrams:

Must meet on matter of extreme urgency. July 17th, Stonewall Hotel, Algiers. Nemeroff.

And all around the globe, in the far-off crime councils, the telegrams were received; men cancelled other appointments and began packing their bags.

And Nemeroff sent a forty-first telegram to a man whose work had highly recommended him. He called him both for his skills and for the impact his presence would have on the leaders from the United States, who were inclined to be suspicious of new ideas. His forty-first telegram went to Jersey City, N.J., to P.J. Kenny.

CHAPTER EIGHT

REMO WALKED INTO THE LOBBY of the Stonewall Hotel. The lobby ran the first three floors of the hotel, crowned by a massive crystal chandelier. Dusky-skinned bellhops skittered around the floor, swarming toward Remo and his small bag like a gang of flies.

He shooed them away and held onto the bag, into which he had put P.J. Kenny's attaché case.

As he had expected, he had had no trouble at customs. The clerk had glanced at the passport in the name of P.K. Johnson, glanced at Remo who was wearing the horn-rimmed glasses as proof of identity, then stamped the passport.

The lobby was empty, which meant that Remo was early. If the expected swarm of criminal leaders had arrived yet, the lobby would be filled with scarred men in silk suits, with white ties and hats, trying to stare each other down, trying to set up their own pecking order of importance. But the lobby was empty.

Almost.

Seated in a chair near the door — facing the desk, reading a newspaper — was a young woman. Her orange knit skirt was too short; it was hiked up high onto her thighs and as Remo scanned the lobby, he could see the tops of her pantyhose.

The woman had dark hair — but brown, not black; her skin was dark too, but it was the darkness of suntan, not race; and her eyes behind giant owl-shaped eyeglasses were a deep green that seemed almost unearthly against the glowing tan face. Instead of lipstick, she wore a whitish kind of lip gloss that was somehow wildly sexy. Her eyes met Remo's briefly, then dropped back to the newspaper page, and a faint smile played at the edges of her lips.

Remo reluctantly removed his eyes and walked to the desk.

The clerk — mustached, with a red fez — moved forward to greet him, smiling oilily. Remo expected him to sound like Groucho Marx.

He did.

"Yes sir, at your service."

Remo spoke loud for the benefit of the girl. "I'm P.J. Kenny. You've got a reservation for me?" In the mirror behind the desk, he saw the girl's eyes lift toward the back of his head.

The clerk looked at a list of names under the desk.

"Oh, yessir; yes indeed; yes, we do. Will the gentleman be staying long?"

"The gentleman may not be staying at all. What's the room like?"

"Oh, very fine, sir."

"Yeah, yeah, I know. Hotel rooms are always very fine." He hoped P.J. Kenny talked like this. "Is there air conditioning?"

"Yes, sir."

"Carpets?"

"Yes, sir," the clerk said, trying unsuccessfully to hide his annoyance at the loudmouthed American.

"I'm sorry if I annoy you," Remo said, "but I'm used to only the best. The finest hotels in Jersey City, New Jersey. I don't stay nowhere but the best."

"This is the very best, sir," the clerk said. He leaned forward. "Your reservations were made by Baron Nemeroff, and any friend of the baron's..." He left the sentence uncompleted, and slammed the silver bell on the desk.

"That's all right," Remo said, waving his hand in dismissal. "Just give me the key."

As he looked up he saw the woman again staring at his back. He wondered if she were interested in him or in the P.J. Kenny he was supposed to be. He'd have to find out.

He chased two bellhops. "All right, kids, I'll do it myself."

"Room 2510," the clerk told him, handing him a brass key with a blue glass ornament attached to it by a chain.

"Okay. And if it's not all right, you'll hear about it," Remo said, taking the key.

Instead of walking to the elevators, he went back across the lobby to the chair where the girl sat. He stopped in front of her, his feet only inches from hers, and she looked up over the newspaper, her eyes bemused under the big circular glasses.

"Yes?"

"I'm sorry, miss, but I'm sure I've seen you somewhere before."

She laughed. "I don't think so," and lowered her eyes to the paper.

"Do you always read newspapers upside down?" he asked.

Her face showed shock, but only momentarily. She recovered quickly and said coldly, "It's not upside down." But the damage had been done. That she was willing to panic for a moment, to think the paper just might be upside down, was proof that it could have been, that she hadn't been reading it. She knew it and Remo knew it.

He smiled at her again, trying to disarm her. "I know it," he said, "but I always say that."

"It must be your Jersey City training in diplomacy, Mr. Kenny." She had volunteered a sentence at last. Her voice was delicately British — not clipped and abrupt, but soft and throaty — and Remo had a letch for the way British women talked.

"One thing I learned in Jersey City diplomacy," he said. "Don't give something for nothing. You know my name and hometown. And I don't know anything about you, except…"

"Except?"

"Except that you're lovely."

She laughed softly. "Well, by all means then, we must maintain the balance of power. My name is Margaret Waters and I'm from London and if you really meant that last compliment, you can call me Maggie."

"A vacationer?" Remo asked.

"An archaeologist. Who would vacation here?"

"People from Jersey City."

She laughed again. "You've just gone down in my esteem."

"If you'll let me buy you dinner, I'll try to recoup my losses. That is, if you don't have a roaring date with Ramses II."

"You know," she said, "you're really much more civilized than you appeared to be when you were abusing that clerk." She pronounced it "clark."

"I've been watching too many gangster movies. Now how about that dinner?"

"I really haven't been able to make contact with Ramses yet. So yes, why not? Shall we make it nine o'clock?"

"Fine. Here?"

"In front of the hotel," she said.

Remo smiled down at her again. He noticed for the first time that her bust was every bit as good as her legs and her face.

"Until then, Maggie," he said, then turned and walked toward the elevators. His trip to Algiers was already a success. The girl was lovely. He was glad now that Chiun had not come; he would have already been harping about Remo's preoccupation with the opposite sex.

He pushed open the door to his room, and stepped into a six-inch deep rug. The entire window wall was of glass, and stepping toward it, Remo could see all of Algiers laid out in front of him, stretching from the hills on the left to the hills faraway on the right. He noticed, too, the small number of lights in the city, compared with an American city.

The bed was set into the floor, and Remo flopped down onto its mattress. It was first rate and hard.

The apartment's living room furniture was off to the left; to the right was a dining table and kitchenette. The air was washed clean and air-conditioned cool. The quarters were better than those he had in the Hotel Palazzo in New York. P.J. Kenny, might he rest in peace, would have approved.

He probably would have approved of Maggie Waters at nine o'clock, too.

Sometimes Remo wished he had not been the recipient of such extensive training, because his initial impulses were all masculine and all correct, but his follow-through gave way to discipline, except in very rare cases.

Trust Chiun, that old torturer. He had managed to take the pleasure out of sex, while taking none of the enjoyment out of the anticipation. It was one of the things for which he'd have to make amends before he went to meet his ancestors, all those earlier Masters of Sinanju.

Remo glanced at his watch. He had not reset it. It was 1:30 New York time. Time to call Smith.

He had the hotel operator start the long routine of an overseas call to Mrs. Martha Cavendish in Secaucus, New Jersey, who if she had existed, would never have realized that she was supposed to be the aunt of Remo Williams.

But as the call was being made, the line would be switched and transferred, and eventually it would find its way to Smith's desk in Folcroft Sanitarium, overlooking Long Island Sound.

It was half an hour before the operator called back.

In heavily accented English that made Remo think she had a scrambler attachment on her mouth, she said, "We have your party."

He heard a click, and said, "Hello."

"Hello," came the nasty lemony voice.

"Uncle Harry?" Remo said. "This is your nephew. I've arrived safely. I just wanted to let you know. I'm in Room 2510 at the Stonewall Hotel in Algiers. Should I call Aunt Martha tomorrow?"

"Yes. Call her at noon."

"Sure. Tell her I'm all right."

"She'd like to hear it herself. Call tomorrow at noon and reassure her."

"Okay if I reverse the charges?" Remo asked.

"Put them on your hotel bill," the puckered voice whined. "How was your trip?"

"All right. There was some snotty guy on the plane. Roger Willis or something. He had an accident."

"Yes, I heard about it. I was worried for a while."

"Nothing to worry about," Remo said. "It was just a perfectly pleasant flight for old P.J. Kenny. Say, Uncle Harry, this is costing money. I'll call tomorrow at noon. Say hello to Ch...to Uncle Charlie."

"I will."

"Be sure. He worries."

"Be sure to call," Smith said.

They both hung up.

Smith would understand why he could not use the scrambler phone. If there was a tap on the line, using the scrambler would be more incriminating than anything he was likely to say.

At any rate, Smith knew his hotel, room and cover name. That should hold him. He hoped Smith would give the message to Chiun. The old Korean was a worrier.

CHAPTER NINE

REMO STOOD IN FRONT OF the Stonewall Hotel, looking along the broad, clean Rue Michelet, the city's main street.

The oppressive heat seemed to coat the city with perspiration. If the humidity could be spooned out to the rest of the world it would end the deserts and turn them into farms. Against the light of the modern, overhanging street lamps, he could see droplets of moisture in the air, sparkling like tiny airborne diamonds.

Remo leaned against a light stanchion, facing the front of the hotel, waiting for Maggie to appear. He wore a white suit, and his hands were stuffed into his jacket pockets as they usually were, which ruined the line of his suits but made him comfortable and therefore, was, in his view, worth doing.

Remo glanced to the side as an auto drove by him, close to the curb, and he caught a glimpse of dark-brown hair in the back seat of a taxi.

He turned to follow the cab with his eyes. It stopped fifty feet down the street from him, under a streetlamp. The back door opened and a long leg slid out. It was Maggie. He recognized the leg, the long recurve from knee to ankle. He looked through the cab's back window. It was Maggie all right. She had stopped — not out, not in — and turned again, and he could see her crisp profile through the window.

She was talking to a man and even at fifty feet, Remo could see his face was hard and lined, his hair so black it was almost blue, like a Superman comic strip.

He was gesturing to Maggie, imperiously, as if he were giving orders and Remo wondered idly who he was. Then she raised her hands toward him in the universal symbol of reluctant agreement, turned again and finished stepping from the cab. With undisguised admiration, Remo watched the long legs; the bust; the face and hair; the smooth, tanned skin. She wore a short, white sleeveless dress, and its contrast made her skin seem darker, healthier.

She smoothed her dress over her buttocks, pressing away wrinkles, then saw Remo watching her. Hurriedly, she shut the cab door, and it sped away. Turning on a smile, she walked toward Remo.

"Hi," she said, throatily.

"Evening. I expected you from inside. That a boyfriend?"

She smiled. "No. The local representative of Ramses II. Had to tell him that I was otherwise engaged this evening."

"You should have held the cab."

"We'll walk," she said. "It's a nice night."

"This is Algiers, honey. We might both wind up being sold into white slavery."

"Mr. Kenny," she began.

"P.J." He wondered, for the first time, what the initials meant.

"P.J.," she said, "with you I'm not worried in the least. Let's walk."

She locked her arm through his and turned to walk off along the street, in the direction away from the taxicab.

"This is the tourist quarter," she said brightly. "There are places not far from here."

"Lead on," he said, "but if you take me to a belly-dancer joint, I'll lose all my respect for you."

"Perish forbid."

He liked her. It felt good to have her hanging on his arm. At times like this, he could almost imagine he was a real person, not someone whose name and fingerprints had vanished from the earth when he met death in the rigged electric chair. No, a real person. With a past, a present and a future, and with a pretty girl on his arm to share it with.

He liked her. It would be a pleasure finding out why she was interested in him, who the man was in the back of the cab, what she knew about Nemeroff and the upcoming meeting and if he had to drag her into bed to work his wicked will on her, why then, he was prepared to make that sacrifice for dear old Smith and CURE.

Smith, Smith, Smith. CURE, CURE, CURE. Three cheers and a tiger. Let's hear it for all professional killers.

Remo Williams. P.J. Kenny. The colonel's lady and Judy O'Grady. Poor P.J. just never had the good sense to go to work for the government.

They walked slowly along the street, arm in arm, not chattering, silently enjoying each other's company like old friends who were sure of each other. A black limousine was parked at the corner a hundred feet ahead, and Remo heard its motor start with the high-pitched shriek of a heavy-duty starter.

Curbside was filled with automobiles and the car pulled out into the roadway, which was empty of traffic, and slowly came down the street toward them. Remo noted the car casually. Strange that its lights were out.

Then he and Maggie were walking along an open stretch of curb where there was a fire hydrant, a street sprinkler and no cars were parked, and the car which had been leisurely coming down the street, suddenly sped up.

The car's back window was open on the sidewalk side and before the car reached them, Remo saw the polished barrel of a gun suddenly extend from the window, gleaming blue and oily in the light of the street lamps. Almost as if it was happening in slow motion, he saw the barrel point toward them.

Remo changed direction in mid-step, pushing himself backwards, his body against Maggie's, bearing her backward, but keeping his body between her and the car. Then they were out of the open area, behind a parked car, and Remo pulled Maggie down with his arm. In one motion, he was on his feet, ready to draw the fire away from Maggie, making himself a target. Bullets started spraying from the passing car now. Bullets by the tens, the dozens, the scores-ignoring Remo, slamming through and over and under the car-toward Maggie. Remo heard them hit with dull thunks into the parked car; he heard them crack crisply off the stone wall behind them; and he cursed the marksman for trying to ruin his night.

He saw a shiny black, hugely-muscled arm holding the submachine gun out the car's window; then he lost his temper and started along the sidewalk, moving toward the front of the parked car which shielded Maggie, ready to go up onto its hood and over onto the roof of the passing limousine.

Crack!

Another bullet hit the stone wall behind him and this time it rebounded upwards and caught Remo in the head as he moved. It felled him. He saw a blue flash, but felt no pain. All he could think of was Chiun, telling him how inept he was not to anticipate a simple ricochet. He put his hand to his right temple, could feel the warm stickiness of blood, and then there was pain, as if he had been slapped by Chiun, as if his head had fallen off, and then he fell back, off the hood of the parked car, onto the sidewalk alongside Maggie.

He woke up, lying on his back on a pleasantly hard mattress.

A girl hovered over him. She was beautiful and *built*. She had wrung out a cloth in a dish of water at a bedside end-table and placed the chilly wet rag on his aching forehead.

He opened his eyes; the girl spoke. She had an English accent. "P.J.? Are you all right?"

"P.J.? he thought. He said, "Yes, I think so. My head hurts."

"Well it might." She wore a white dress and was really lovely, tanned with deep brown hair and the brightest of green eyes. He hoped she was not just a nurse. He hoped she was someone he knew well. Maybe a wife or a girlfriend.

"What happened?" he said.

"You don't remember?"

"I don't remember anything."

"We were walking down the street and someone fired shots at you. A bullet grazed your temple."

"Someone fired shots at me?"

"Yes."

"Why would anyone do that?"

"I don't know," she said. "I thought you might."

"I don't know anything," he said. He sat up in bed, ignoring the throb of pain in his temple, and looked around the room. It was a hotel room, luxuriously furnished. For some reason, he wondered who was paying for it.

"What is this place?" he asked.

"You're teasing me."

"No, I'm not." His tone was sincere and truthful, and quietly she answered: "This is the Stonewall Hotel in Algiers. Your room."

"Algiers?" he said in astonishment. "What am I doing in Algiers?" He paused for a long moment, obviously thinking hard. "Who am I, anyway?"

She stared at him for a full ten seconds. Then she removed the cloth from his head and looked at the wound.

"It doesn't seem too bad," she said. "Just a small bandage job."

"You didn't answer my question," he said. "Who am I?"

"Your name is P.J. Kenny."

It meant nothing to him. "And this is Algiers?"

"Yes."

"What am I doing here?"

"I don't know."

He looked around the room again. Knowing your name was no good at all, not unless it had some convenient handles of memory attached to it. His had none.

"Who is P.J. Kenny?" he asked.

"You are."

"No, I don't mean that. Really, who am I? What do I do? What am I all about?"

"You really don't know?"

"No, I don't."

She stood up and walked away from the bed. He sank back onto the pillows. Sudden movements hurt some, but he could not resist turning slightly on the pillow so he could watch her as she walked away. She was exquisite. But who was she?

At the foot of the bed, she turned and looked at him, leaning forward on the edge of the bed.

"I don't know who you are either," she said. "We just met. But you lie there and I'll look around the room. Perhaps I can find something to help. You've got amnesia."

"Amnesia! I thought that was just a hypnotist's trick."

"No," she said. "It's real enough. I used to be a nurse. I've seen many cases of it. Fortunately, it's generally only a matter of a few hours."

He grinned. "I'll wait it out if you promise to stay with me."

"I'd better look around," she said. She started with the dresser drawers. Expertly, she rifled them, looking under and behind each piece of clothing, between the individual garments. She felt the inside of his socks. Nothing.

In the bottom drawer, she found an attaché case. She pulled it out, put it on the dresser and unsnapped the lock. Remo watched her with interest, admiring her technique.

She hummed slightly as she looked through the case. He could see her hands moving. What was she doing? It hurt, but he got to his feet and walked to her side.

The attaché case held money, piles of hundred-dollar bills. He would guess the total at $25,000.

"I already like being P.J. Kenny," he said.

"There's a telegram here, too," she said, pulling out a yellow sheet.

"Read it."

"It's addressed to P.J. Kenny, Hotel Divine, Jersey City, N.J. 'Register at the Stonewall Hotel. Reservations made for you. Look forward to fruitful business relationship. Nemeroff.'"

"Who's Nemeroff?"

She hesitated, just a fraction of a second too long. "I don't know," she said. "But he's probably why you're here."

She walked away from him, and opened his closet, to look through his clothes. He went to follow; then, from the corner of his eye, saw his reflection in the mirror. He turned and looked into the glass.

It was the face of a stranger staring at him. A bad face. Not just the ugly-looking gash on his temple, but something else. His hair was short cropped and wavy. His eyes were hard and relentless looking; his lips long and thin. The face looked as if it were skin over bone, as if the flesh had been omitted. P.J. Kenny was not a nice man. He knew that.

He leaned forward toward the mirror, looking closer. There was something else, too. He raised his fingertips to his cheekbone. The skin was a little too thin, as if it had been stretched taut. At the corners of his eyes, the skin had the same feel. Plastic surgery. He knew it. Without a doubt, he knew it.

She had finished her inspection of the closet, and she watched him as he examined his face.

"Well?" she said, with humor in her voice. "Do you pass?"

"It's odd. Looking at yourself and seeing a stranger. Did you find anything?" he said, shaking his head in puzzlement and returning to the bed.

She followed him, her hand at her side, hidden from view. He sat on the bed and she stood before him.

"Just this," she said.

She extended her hand toward him. She held a stiletto. He could tell the blade was razor sharp.

He took the knife from her and laid it on his palm. It was eight inches in length and it had a professional feel to it, but it was a feel that seemed foreign to him. He turned it around in his hand, looking at the twin, razor-sharp sides of the blade, turning it over-first handle, then blade, then handle again and then, without thinking, raised it over his head and let it fly at the wooden hotel door.

The knife transcribed one lazy, half-turn, flashing across the room, and then hit the door, chest high, point first, and it tore through the thin plywood covering of the hollow door, burying itself two inches deep along its blade before stopping. It hung there, imbedded, its handle quivering slightly.

The girl looked at it, then turned her eyes back to him. He watched the knife until it stopped vibrating, then smiled up at her.

"At last," he said, "I know who I am."

"Oh?"

"Yeah. I'm a knife thrower in the goddamn circus. I don't even know how I did that."

The girl sat on the edge of the bed and her dress hiked up on her thighs, revealing a lot of well-turned, well-tanned leg. She took her hands in his.

"It's apparent," she said, "that only this Nemeroff, whoever he is, will be able to clear up your identity. I'm going to go out for a few minutes and see if I can find out anything about Nemeroff. Who he is.

Where he is. Then we can figure out what to do." She squeezed his hands gently. "Will you be all right for a few minutes?"

"Without you? I don't know."

She leaned forward and kissed him on the bridge of the nose. "I'll make it up to you when I get back," she said.

"Then hurry."

"I will." Then she was on her feet and out the door, closing it tight behind her, and as the door closed, the knife quivered again, and he lay there, looking at it, wondering just what kind of man he was to be able to throw a knife like that.

CHAPTER TEN

MAGGIE WATERS JABBED IMPATIENTLY AT the elevator button, and while waiting, nervously tapped the sole of one high-heeled white shoe on the heavy beige carpeting in the hallway of the twenty-fifth floor of the Stonewall Hotel.

After what seemed an interminably long time, the elevator came, opened, and Maggie stepped in. She rode down to the twelfth floor, and with a key from her handbag opened the door to Room 1227.

She glanced around the room, which she now found distasteful after having been in Remo's room. Hers was like a cheap Alabama motel room, with linoleum tile floors, and thin drapes, and mica-finished furniture. She closed the door behind her, pressing it tightly, since she had noticed that it was warped and stuck, unlocked, in the dampness that pervaded the halls of the lower floors of the Stonewall.

Inside, she walked to the phone and dialed four short digits.

"Yes," a voice answered. It was a British male voice, professionally bored, and for some reason, it annoyed her as much as her room. The sun was indeed setting on the empire. Sensible people would prepare for night. The British had too much tradition to be sensible. They went on, unconcerned, and each one acted as if he were King Arthur.

"Maggie here," she said.

"Oh, yes," the man said. "What's new? How's the boyfriend?"

"The boyfriend took a bullet in the head," she said, viciously happy to be overstating the case, to see what reaction she could draw from the man on the other end of the telephone.

"Oh," he said.

She pursed her lips. "But he's all right," she said, after a pause. "Just a flesh wound. Now, dammit, he's suffering from amnesia. He doesn't know who he is."

"I say, that's interesting. What about Nemeroff?"

"He's never heard of him. I tried the name on for size."

"That's a piquant turn of affairs, isn't it?" the man said. "The baron hires a professional killer and now the killer not only doesn't know the baron, he doesn't even know that he's a killer."

If he chuckled, she thought she would die.

He chuckled.

"Yes," she said. "Very piquant."

"Yes, indeed," he said.

"Yes, indeed," she parroted. "But what happens when Nemeroff comes for him?"

"Well, my dear, that may very well be your entree to the baron's company." He chuckled again. "You can pose as P.J. Kenny's private nurse. Would you like to play nurse with him?" he asked, his voice attenuated in the spoken equivalent of a leer.

"I would presume," she said coldly, "that it would be safer to play nurse with him than it would with you. He probably does not have a dose."

The man's voice sputtered slightly. "It was in the line of duty, Maggie."

"It's amazing how you're always running into five shilling whores in the line of duty. The top agent in her majesty's secret service." It was an accusation.

"The hazards of the trade," he said. "You should not forget that my discomfiture has given you the opportunity to carry out this mission and make your own reputation."

"Should I thank you or your trollop?"

"Thanks are not necessary," he said. "At any rate, see if you can get to Nemeroff through P.J. Kenny. The Scambia plan must be stopped at all costs. Stop Nemeroff. And if that appears impossible…"

"Yes?"

"If that appears impossible," he repeated, "kill P.J. Kenny."

She did not answer for a moment and he went on: "When his memory returns, and it will, he will kill you in a minute. He is a vicious cold-blooded maniac with a knife. If you must, kill him before he kills you. Don't hesitate." Then, he said: "Oh, I wish I were on this case instead of you."

"I wish you were too," she said.

"Unfortunately...my physical condition..." He left the rest of the sentence unspoken.

"Imagine," she said. "The secret service laid low by the clap."

"To hell with the service." He chuckled sardonically. "I was laid low."

"You are always laid low," she said. "Ta, ta. Don't forget your penicillin."

"Be careful," he said. "Remember, this is important. The stakes are mortal. An international crime empire stands in the balance. Nothing can be more important than stopping the evil Baron Nemeroff and his nefarious scheme. Nothing. Not your life. Not mine. Not..."

"Save it for your next book," she said, and hung up.

She looked at the telephone for a long minute after replacing it, then shrugged, and headed back toward the door. All right. To hell with it. She was an agent, and she would do what her boss had told her to do. There was no room for emotionalism in her trade.

But to herself she smiled. She relished the prospect of looking in on P.J. Kenny and she looked forward to the opportunity to play nurse with him.

And Great Britain's top agent be damned. May his next dose be fatal.

CHAPTER ELEVEN

DR. HAROLD W. SMITH TWISTED around in his swivel chair, studied the waters of Long Island Sound, and felt sorry for himself.

Remo was overdue. He was supposed to have called at noon. He glanced at his watch. Two hours ago. Two hours in CURE could be an eternity. Five minutes of knowing Remo Williams could seem like an eternity.

He could have guessed that the wise bastard wouldn't call. Why did Remo Williams have to be a wise guy?

Why did he have to work for Dr. Harold W. Smith?

Why did Smith have to run CURE? Why did there have to be a CURE?

God, I feel sorry for me, he thought, as he continued to ask himself the unfamiliar questions, questions he had not really considered in the years he had headed the nation's most secret organization.

Smith was the quintessential bureaucrat. Given a task of the utmost stupidity, he would perform it capably. He would not worry about the innate stupidity of it.

Of course, he was the ultimate bureaucrat, but with a difference. First, he was intelligent. Second, he was honest. Third, he was an absolute patriot.

Patriotism was sometimes the last refuge of scoundrels who hid themselves by wrapping themselves in the flag. But Smith wrapped himself around the flag to protect it and shield it. So the simple fact was that when a President made a judgment that CURE was necessary in the fight against lawlessness, there was only one man in the government with the background, the honesty, the patriotism, the espionage skills, the administrative know-how, to run it. Dr. Harold W. Smith.

And that was many years ago, and here he was, near pension age, but he knew now there would never be a pension, his children were grown now and he had missed their childhoods, and he was denied even the usual out of the wayward parent: the right to tell his now-grown children, well, this is the way it was and that's why I couldn't be there. Even that was denied him.

With a conscious effort of will, he forced the whole package of resentment out of his mind. His problem now was — *where was Remo?*

He had not called from Algiers, and despite his antics, missing a check-in was something Remo did not do. Somehow, it had penetrated even through Remo's thick skull that missing a call-in might trigger whole series of events and actions that, once started, would be impossible to call off. So he always called. But today he hadn't and he was two hours overdue.

That meant trouble. Smith had no faith in the ability of the secret agencies of other countries to stop Nemeroff. He had regarded it as CURE's assignment, as America's problem. He had assigned his biggest weapon, Remo Williams, and given him a free hand, hoping that that free hand would be used to kill Nemeroff.

Nemeroff's name had moved through the CURE crime computers too many times and Smith, probably better than any other man in the world, had a fair idea of the full extent of the baron's illegal influence. The world would be better rid of him. And Scambia would be better off without its assassination-minded vice president, Asiphar.

He had hoped that that solution would occur to Williams. But now, as the minutes had lengthened into hours and Remo had not called, he began to worry that somehow the solution had become part of the problem.

He watched the waters of the sound for a few minutes longer, then picked up the telephone and gave his secretary a number to call.

In a few minutes, the buzzer rang. He picked up the phone, prepared for his country's sake, to perform a distasteful service.

"Hello, Chiun. This is Doctor Smith."

"Yes," Chiun said. How many times had Smith spoken to him on the phone; how many times had Chiun responded merely, "yes?" It was like talking to a wall.

"I have not heard from your student," Smith said.

"Nor have I."

"He has missed his noon check-in."

"That is apparent if you have not heard from him," Chiun said.

"What was his mood when he left?"

"If you mean, has he fled from you, the answer is no."

"Are you sure?" Smith asked.

"I am sure," Chiun said. "I informed him of a great honor soon to be his. He would not now flee."

"Perhaps he's drunk some place?" Smith suggested.

"I think not," Chiun suggested.

And then, because there was simply nothing left to say by either of them, each hung up. Neither thought to say goodbye.

Smith depressed the receiver with his finger, then called his secretary again. Within a minute, he had set in motion procedures to quietly check upon the whereabouts of a P.J. Kenny who was registered at the Stonewall Hotel in Algiers.

The sun was beginning to dip over the sound when the answer came back. Mr. P.J. Kenny is still registered at the Stonewall Hotel in Algiers. On the previous evening, he was wounded in some sort of shooting incident. The extent of his injuries is unknown, since no doctor was called into attendance, and he has not yet left his room.

"Thank you," Smith said. Then, himself, without his secretary, dialed the number of the Hotel Palazzo in New York. He must seek Chiun's advice.

The hotel operator answered.

"Room Eleven-eleven," Smith said.

The operator hesitated a moment, then Smith heard a phone ringing.

"Front desk," came a man's voice.

"I asked for Room Eleven-eleven," Smith said, annoyance leaking from his voice.

"Whom did you wish to speak to?" the clerk asked.

"Mr. Park. The elderly Oriental gentleman."

"I'm sorry, sir, but Mr. Park has left word that he will be gone for a few days."

"He has? Did he say where he was going?"

"As a matter of fact, he did. He said he was going to Algeria."

"Thank you," Smith said slowly, and hung up. Well, that was that. Remo had called Chiun, told him he needed help, and Chiun was on his way. Nothing to do but wait.

And at the front desk of the Hotel Palazzo, a young, blond-haired clerk looked into the hazel eyes of a wizened old Oriental, who smiled at him.

"You have performed me most valuable services," Chiun said.

"It was a pleasure to serve you," the clerk said.

"It is a pleasure equally as great to meet a servant who understands that his function is to serve," Chiun said. "You have made my flight reservation?"

"Yes."

"And my steamer trunks will get to the airport on time?"

"Yes."

"And a taxicab is waiting for me?"

"Yes."

"You have indeed done well," Chiun said. "I must show you my appreciation."

"No sir," the clerk said, waving a hand at Chiun, in whose hand a small money-purse had magically appeared. "No sir. Just doing my job," he said, wishing it were not the policy of the hotel and that he could accept whatever gratuity this wealthy old looney-tune were about to force upon him.

Chiun hesitated.

"No sir," the clerk said again, less vigorously this time.

Chiun snapped his purse closed again. "As you will," he said, feeling rather good about it. A quarter saved was a quarter earned.

Two hours later, Chiun, with the passport in the name of C.H. Park, was aboard a jetliner heading for Algiers. He sat quietly in a window seat, looking out at the bright afternoon clouds. His whole life was spent in doing errands, it seemed. Like now. Going across half the earth to chide Remo for not calling in on time.

Only fleetingly did it occur to Chiun that Remo might be in some kind of trouble. He dismissed the thought as quickly as it came. After all, was not Remo the embodiment of Shiva, the Destroyer? Was he not Chiun's pupil? Would he not be the Master of Sinanju one day? What could happen to such a one?

CHAPTER TWELVE

THE MAN WHO THOUGHT HE WAS P.J. Kenny had been unable to remember anything at all from his past. Even if he had, he was sure it would not be nearly as pleasant as his present.

He had inspected his wallet the night before while the English girl was out of the room. It contained $4,000. Except for a passport made out in the name of P.K. Johnson, which was obviously a phony, he had no papers, no indication of just who or what P.J. Kenny was, no reason for anyone to have pegged shots at him. Just the telegram from Baron Nemeroff, whoever he was.

Then the English girl was back and he lost all interest in Nemeroff. She was Maggie Waters, she was a British archaeologist, he had picked her up in the hotel lobby and she seemed to think that she had some obligation to make love to him. As Englishmen everywhere, she discharged her obligation.

So did he. Over and over. Through the night. Into the second day. On and on. P.J. Kenny, whoever he was, was quite a man. He knew tricks she had never seen before; things to do with his fingers and his lips and his knees that reduced her to jelly, to babbling insensibility; that drove her to peaks of pleasure that were unbearably intense. And then he made them even more intense.

He taught her a new position called the Yokohama YoYo and a new technique called the Capistrano Swallow and he denied having learned them from an American book, called the Sensuous Pervert.

"Be quiet and keep working," he said.

So she labored. Winston Churchill, he thought, would have been proud of her.

They had breakfasted in bed, and lunched in bed and were on their way toward dinner in bed.

"It was never like this," she said.

"I don't know if it was ever like this or not," he said. "But I doubt it."

"I know now you're not a knife thrower."

"What am I?" he asked.

She put her face close to his ear and told him.

"Maybe that's just my hobby," he said. "Maybe knife throwing's my profession."

"Then you're in the wrong trade," she said.

"Can I give your name as a recommendation?" he asked.

"You'll never need one."

"Thank you," he said and put his lips over hers.

Then the door was flung open as if it had not been locked. In the doorway stood a black giant, wearing pantaloons and a vest without a shirt. His muscles dripped muscles. He was six-foot-five and weighed at least 250 pounds. The red fez on his head made him seem even taller; linebackers would have thought twice before tackling him.

He stood in the doorway, a bulging lump of glistening black power, his white eyes shining out of the darkness of his face, looking with disinterest at Remo and Maggie.

Remo rolled on his back and looked at him as Maggie pulled the sheet over her. Then Remo said:

"You made a mistake, pal. You swam ashore too soon. The Empire State Building is 5,000 miles that way." He jerked a thumb toward what he considered to be west. "Call us if you need help fighting off the aircraft attack."

The black stood there impassively, his big white eyes taking in the scene slowly.

The man who thought he was P.J. Kenny got out of bed and padded, naked, toward the door to slam it in the big buck's face.

Then the black spoke. "You P.J. Kenny?" Remo laughed aloud. The man's voice was high pitched and musical, higher pitched than a woman's. He sounded like a munchkin, a six-foot-five, 250-pound munchkin.

Still laughing, Remo said: "That's me."

"Baron Nemeroff wants you." He spoke precise English but the voice was pure soprano.

"About time," Remo said. Good, he thought. Time to find out just who he was and where he had come from.

He turned toward his closet. Maggie, shamelessly, had gotten up from bed. She walked naked across the floor, without embarrassment, head high, shoulders back, breasts erect. "Let's go, P.J.," she said, "we don't want to keep the baron waiting." She had her dress on then, was raising it over her head and then sliding it down her arms, aided by a wiggle that Remo decided was exceptionally sexy. He felt outraged that she might have hid it from him. He wondered if Nemeroff, whoever he was, would mind waiting.

He asked the black.

"The baron wants you now," the black said.

Remo shrugged. "I thought as much." He went to the closet and got out slacks and shirt, and dressed quickly. He wore white tennis shoes without socks, a new European glove-leather type that did not make the feet sweaty. Maggie leaned over the dresser, putting lipstick on. While all this was going on, the black stood motionless in the doorway, like a lawn ornament. He needed a lamp, Remo thought.

"Let's go, P.J.," Maggie said cheerily. The black took a step into the room and held up his hand in the traffic policeman's universal gesture for stop. "Not you," he said. "The Baron wants only him."

"But I'm his constant companion," Maggie said. "We go everywhere together."

"Not you."

Remo was listening to the words with only half his mind. The black's upraised arm had bunched his bicep into a huge lump and it glistened bluish in the sunlight coming through the windows. It bit at Remo's mind, that somewhere he had seen just such a giant black arm as that, someplace just recently. But he could not remember where.

A cold stare passed between Maggie and the black. Remo stepped into the chill.

"That's all right, Maggie," he said. "I'll go alone. And I'll get right back to you. I promise."

Remo glanced at his reflection next to Maggie's in the dresser mirror. He looked all right. Except for a small bandage on his temple, there was no sign of his wounding last night. He had no headaches, no pain, no problems — except the biggest one. He didn't know who he was.

Where had he learned to throw a knife like that? And make love like that? Maybe he was an international white slaver? Well, there were worse ways of making a living, he supposed. Baron Nemeroff might be able to straighten it out.

Then Maggie was in his arms, her arms around his neck, kissing him hard, and then nuzzling her face against his neck. She whispered into his ear: "P.J., be careful. Nemeroff's dangerous. I can't tell you anything, but don't let on about your amnesia."

He held her away from him. "Don't worry about a thing," he said, smiling. So she knew more about him than she'd let on. Okay, he'd get that out of her when he came back. In the meantime, it was on to Baron Nemeroff.

"Let's go, son of Kong," he said, brushing past the black and out into the hallways.

The black did not move and in the hallway Remo turned to see what was delaying him. He saw the huge man place a big hand against Maggie's chest and push her backwards onto the bed, then stand there looking at her. Even from the side, Remo could see the smile that lit the black's face. It was a smile of evil hatred, not of lust but of something stronger than lust. Maggie lay on the bed, a look of fright on her face. The black stepped toward her. He put his hand on the wooden post at the end of the bed and made as if to climb over it onto the bed after her. Then a knife whizzed into the wood of the bed post, between his fingers. It stuck there quivering. The black froze, and then turned to the doorway.

Remo's arm was just returning to his side. "The next time, Rastus," he said, coldly, "it'll be in your throat."

The black's saucer eyes glared at Remo. For a moment, he seemed on the verge of charging, then he dropped his hands quietly to his sides and walked past Remo out into the hall, striding purposefully toward the elevators.

As Remo closed the door, he told Maggie: "Call the desk and get this door lock fixed. There may be more of these things around," he said, jerking his head in the direction of the black escort.

Then he turned and followed him.

CHAPTER THIRTEEN

"LISTEN, ALI BABA. IF YOU ever want to come to the States, you can make a fortune as a cab driver. Imagine. A cab driver who doesn't talk."

"And with that costume you could get all the gay trade, running to their latest liberation rally so they can squeak at each other. Man, I'll tell you. You'd be a winner."

Having divested himself of that opinion, the man who thought he was P.J. Kenny leaned back in the passenger's seat in the Mercedes Benz limousine, enjoying the scenery.

The black had not spoken since they had left Remo's room in the Stonewall Hotel. Remo had kept up a stream of chatter. He knew he had some reason to dislike the black; he just didn't know what it was. He knew he disliked him even more after he manhandled Maggie. That was one Remo owed him. Was P.J. Kenny a vindictive man? The man who thought he was P.J. Kenny hoped so.

Algiers is a long, busy city, stretching from hills on the left to hills on the right. The Stonewall Hotel was located on the city's main street, the Rue Michelet, which undergoes two name changes as it winds its way up to the hills on the eastern end of the city. The streets were lined with dwarf evergreens and were spotlessly clean. But they were still all roads leading from nowhere to nowhere. Maybe P.J. Kenny was a poet.

They were moving now toward the crests of the hills, and then the black turned off the main paved road, onto a dirt road, and up ahead, atop a hill that looked down over Algiers, Remo could see a massive castle, white against the white sky, its windows massive cutouts in stone. A touch of Transylvania, Remo thought.

He leaned back again in the seat, looking around him. Up ahead, he saw a helicopter flying lazy circles around the castle, like a housefly looking for a sweet landing-spot.

And there was another helicopter on the roof, its rotor barely visible from this angle.

So Baron Nemeroff had his own air force. It wasn't much, Remo thought, but in an all-out war, it could probably lick the whole Algerian army. Come to think of it, the whole Pan-Arab Union.

Remo looked out the side window at the heavy undergrowth that licked its way up to the road's edge. He saw an armed man wearing hunting clothes walking through the brush. But he was no hunter — not unless hunters had begun to use machine guns.

On the other side of the car, it was the same, Remo noticed. Men moving through the brush, heavily armed men. Remo's eyes glanced down again at the huge black bicep of the driver, as he flexed it while steering the hard-sprung limousine over the bumpy road. The sight of the arm raised a tingle in Remo's head; something he should remember, but couldn't. He had seen that arm before. Oh well, he would remember it eventually. Maybe Baron Nemeroff would tell him.

It would be interesting to find out who P.J. Kenny was. He knew the amnesia would wear off soon, but he wanted to know now who and what he was, what he did, and what he was doing here. Maggie had warned him to be careful.

The narrow road, already wide enough for only one car, suddenly became even narrower, and then, as they turned a curve, they came to a gatehouse.

Two armed men stood in the roadway, rifles folded in the crooks of their arms, but they moved aside when they recognized the car and driver. Without slowing, the black sped between the two men, and then the road lifted sharply upward and they neared Nemeroff's castle.

At that same moment, a huge jet appeared over the castle, coming in for a landing at the Algiers airport. Remo glanced at it and wondered what kind of people would come to Algeria if they didn't have to.

The Mercedes spit up gravel as it swerved again, and then it was pulling into a large opened area, at the bottom of stone steps leading up to the first floor level patio of the castle. The parking area was paved with flagstones of different colors and there was room for fifty or sixty autos to park there. The black jammed on the brakes and seemed disappointed when Remo did not go through the windshield. He turned off the motor, got out and headed up the steps toward the patio, crooking a finger at Remo, motioning him to follow.

Remo left the car and walked up the broad stairway to the patio. Its deck was cut from rough unfinished marble and it looked like a Parisian outdoor restaurant, with clusters of small, black wrought-iron tables, each with two chairs at it. At the side of the patio, sliding glass doors opened into what appeared to be a large study, and from the patio, more stone stairs rose outdoors to a second floor, where there was another balconied patio.

"You wait here," the black squeaked in his high-pitched voice, which brought a grin from Remo.

Remo perched himself on the stone wall surrounding the patio and looked out over the grounds. His eyes spotted more men out in the underbrush, all armed, all in hunter's garb, and from the good vantage point, Remo could see them talking to each other over walkie-talkie radios. They seemed to be in four waves; two rows of men on the far side of the gatehouse which blocked the only road, and two rows of men working closer toward the castle. They worked back and forth in a zippering kind of search action, which Remo somehow, instinctively, knew was highly disciplined and highly effective.

Then he heard the whoosh of the glass door opening, and then steps on the patio behind him.

He turned.

The man coming toward him was almost seven feet tall. He was stringy, but his greyhound stride, the angles of his face, his mannerisms, all exuded power. There was strength in his grip, too, as he reached forward and grabbed Remo's hand in his own and began to pump it up and down.

He looked searchingly into Remo's face, his own face wearing a slight questioning look. Then he stared some more at Remo.

He knows, Remo thought. He knows I'm not Kenny.

Then he smiled, his big horse-face breaking into a humorless grin, and said, "Mr. Kenny, well, well. I'm Baron Nemeroff."

So they had never met.

"Glad to be here," Remo said, smiling.

"The plastic surgery is excellent," Nemeroff said. "You look nothing like your photographs." Proof they had never met.

"That was the idea," Remo said, hoping that that indeed had been the idea.

"I trust you had a good trip. Namu did not misbehave in any way?"

"Namu?"

"My eunuch," Nemeroff said.

"So that's it. I thought he was on leave from the Mormon Tabernacle Choir."

Nemeroff smiled weakly. "No. It is an ancient custom of the land. To emasculate one's manservant."

"Then how do you sleep at night?" Remo asked. "Knowing he's loose and what you did to him?"

"It's strange, perhaps, to us. But a eunuch's devotion to his master is absolute. It becomes almost a form of worship. Perhaps the loss of their own masculinity makes them seek out others' masculinity. Who is more masculine than the man who mutilated them?"

"Who indeed?"

He clapped Remo on the back. "But enough of that. Come join me in a pre-dinner snack."

He turned and walked toward the nearest table, slapping his hands together once with a report like a pistol shot. He sat, and gestured that Remo sit at the table, too but before Remo was in the seat, a male servant, dressed in butler's garb, appeared on the patio, bearing a silver tray, laden with food.

Remo sat in the wrought-iron chair and watched the food being unpiled from the tray. There was a wicker basket of rolls and even before the basket stopped vibrating on the table, Nemeroff had seized a roll, thrust it into his mouth, tearing off a large chunk and chewing animatedly.

He called the meal a snack. It included soup, salad, a rare steak — no, make that two rare steaks — milk, yogurt, shrimp salad, and coffee laced heavily with cream and sugar.

The baron had attacked the first roll in what seemed to be a piranhic frenzy. But now he was calmer and as the butler stood there, he asked Remo: "What will you have?" slightly accenting the "you," making it clear that the food on the table now was the baron's own ration.

The sight of the food had made Remo hungry. The sky was the limit, he knew. Any kind of food. Why did he lust for food?

He hesitated, and Nemeroff said: "Our larder is well stocked, Mr. Kenny. Just name your wish. Steak. Frogs' legs. Hummingbirds? Lobster. Caviar. Your desire."

And without knowing why, Remo said: "Rice." Then, because he did not want to seem ungracious, "and a piece of boiled fish."

The butler looked startled. "Boiled fish, sir?"

"Yes. Trout, if you have it. If not, haddock will do. Nothing oily. And do not season the rice."

The butler gave the closest thing to a shrug that a butler could give. "Very good, sir." He walked away.

Nemeroff was now deep into his soup, slopping it up from a bowl in a large spoon. Drops fell from his spoon, but the spoon seemed to be on a treadmill, from the bowl to Nemeroff's mouth, continuously, and the spoon seemed to get back to the bowl even before the spilled drops did.

"Strange diet," Nemeroff hissed, then swallowed. "Rice and fish." Another spoonful. "Still..." Another spoonful. "I guess...You know... What you like."

He looked up as if waiting for agreement,

Remo nodded, smiling.

The rice and fish returned in ten minutes. By that time, Nemeroff's eating frenzy seemed to have waned, and he contented himself with picking at his food, leaning back in his chair expansively. He said, "I'm really glad you could come. I trust the financial arrangements were satisfactory."

"Yes, very," Remo thought, remembering the $25,000 in his briefcase.

"So now as you eat, let me tell you why you are here," Nemeroff said. He picked up his coffee cup and saucer in his left hand then raised the cup to his mouth, and slurped a noisy mouthful.

Remo spooned silently through his rice. It was white rice; he preferred brown. At least, he thought he did. He could not even remember liking rice.

"You are here," Nemeroff said, "for several reasons. The first, frankly, is because of your reputation in your country. I think that will guarantee the close attention of your countrymen...who share our profession." He slurped and Remo wanted to shout, "What profession?"

"The second reason you are here is of a much more immediate nature. There are people in Algiers now who would do anything to stop our plan from going into operation. It would be your responsibility to stop them, if you decide to join with me."

Remo looked up and nodded, hoping the nod was not too equivocal. It sounded like P.J. Kenny was a professional assassin. Balls, that was no fun. He had hoped that he managed a Playboy Club somewhere.

Maybe he was way off base. Maybe it was a circus act. There was Namu, the strong man, and Nemeroff, the stilt-walker and P.J. Kenny, the knife-thrower.

Nemeroff, for the first time, noticed the bandage on Remo's temple. "What happened?" he asked. "I hope you're not hurt."

"No," Remo said. "A little incident last night. Somebody pegged shots at me in front of the hotel."

"Oh, dear. That's too bad. It means someone knows you're here and is already afraid of your presence."

"Occupational hazard," Remo said, hoping that was the right thing to say.

"Yes, indeed," Nemeroff agreed. He was finally finished with his coffee. He wiped his mouth with a napkin.

"You perhaps are wondering why I have not mentioned money, Mr. Kenny," Nemeroff said. "Frankly, I wanted to see you at first hand before I committed myself. But now I am quite sure." He leaned forward and placed his elbows on the table, his horse face staring ahead at Remo's. "I want you to be more than just an employee," he said. "I want you to be a partner in this little enterprise."

"Why me?" Remo asked, carefully chewing a piece of the boiled trout.

"Have you ever heard of Nimzovich?" Nemeroff asked.

"A chess player," Remo said, wondering why he knew that.

Indeed," Nemeroff said, "He once mentioned a 'passed pawn's lust to expand.' In setting up my plan to make the nation of Scambia a haven for criminals from all over the world, the one lingering problem has been your nation's Mafia and its own 'lust to expand.' I could readily see how, within months, I would be fighting off your nation's criminal interests who would try to seize the nation of Scambia for their own purposes. While this would not be difficult for me to do, it would be time-consuming and troublesome, and I did not want this kind of trouble."

"Of course not," Remo agreed.

"So I began to look around," Nemeroff said. "And everywhere, I ran across your name." He raised a hand to silence any show of modesty that might be coming. None was.

"You are trusted in your country," Nemeroff said. "Even more important, you are feared. With you on the scene in Scambia, all from your nation will know that it is, how do you say, on the level. And with you on the scene, no one will attempt any takeover. In addition, Vice President Asiphar of Scambia will perform much more creditably, I believe, if he knows I have an agent there who would not hesitate to take the most extreme measures, should Asiphar fail us. And finally, there is of course, your own personal interests. You are, I understand, being sought in your own country now. This would be an opportunity for you to start life afresh. Untold wealth and power could be yours. You could be almost a king." He looked at Remo and his horse face asked questions.

Remo put down his fork. "You mentioned wealth. How much wealth?"

Nemeroff guffawed. "A practical man. I like that. Ten percent of all that comes into Scambia is yours."

"And that would be?"

"Millions a year," Nemeroff said. "Millions."

So he was a professional assassin and now he was being offered the jackpot. Strange, it produced no outrage in the man who thought he was P.J. Kenny, no sense of revulsion. Just a calm acceptance of his role in life. It was as if he had been created to destroy. But he wished he knew more about the techniques of assassination.

"Earlier, you said that it would be my job now to stop some people who are interested in stopping us. What people?" Remo asked, sipping tea without lemon or sugar.

"I take it then that you agree to my proposition?"

"I do."

Nemeroff stood up and again extended his hand, pumping Remo's. "Good," he said. "Your partnership is all we need for success. And now let us go to my storeroom. You may find some useful weapons in my arsenal there, and we will discuss the necessary housekeeping problems that you will have to resolve in the next several days."

The arsenal was in the basement of the castle, and Nemeroff and Remo reached it by elevator from the main floor. They stopped outside a locked iron door, and while Nemeroff fumbled on a ring looking for the key, Remo could smell the firecracker odor of cordite. Somehow, it was a familiar smell.

They stepped through the gate and Nemeroff touched a light switch. The room was bathed in a soft, glareless light from long fluorescent lights, hidden behind diffusion panels high up on the walls.

The room they stood in was fifty feet long and equally wide; it looked to Remo like a bowling alley. But instead of wooden highways, leading to wooden pins, the room was broken up by low walls, separating the room into six, long, thin slices. At the end of each slice was a life-sized dummy of a man.

"My shooting gallery," Nemeroff said. "And my weapons are here." He opened the door to another room and flicked on the light. Rack after rack of machine guns, automatic rifles, bazookas, pistol display cases, knifes, swords, bolos, machetes, all met Remo's eyes.

"Equipped for anything," Remo said.

"Actually," Nemeroff said, "this is just hobby material for me. I have a factory in West Germany which provides, on demand, any large store of weaponry I might require. But go ahead, test the merchandise."

Remo went to one of the wall racks and looked at the handguns. They were clean and oiled; there was not a trace of dust on any of them. From the rack, he selected a .357 Magnum and a German Luger. He hefted the Luger in his hand, then replaced it on the rack and took down a .38 caliber Smith and Wesson police revolver. It had a familiar feel as he balanced it in his hand.

"My own favorites, exactly," Nemeroff said. "Come. The

ammunition is at the firing line. You must show me your proficiency."

He took Remo by the elbow and led him back to the first of the six gun stalls. He pressed a button on the side of the stall and a panel in its polished Formica surface slid back, revealing racks of ammunition.

"Help yourself," he said.

"Everything for the tourist," Remo said.

"Yes, of course," He settled himself into a seat five feet away from the loading table and watched as Remo drew careful aim on the stuffed dummy at the other end, holding the Magnum carefully at arm's length. Remo squeezed the trigger. The shot felt true. The dummy shuddered as the slug hit. Above the figure of the dummy, outlined on the wall, came another silhouette of the dummy. A flashing red light on the silhouette, just below the heart, showed where Remo's bullet had gone.

"Good shot," Nemeroff said. "Particularly with someone else's weapon."

Remo was somehow annoyed that he had missed the heart. He realized that he was wrong to aim, but he did not know why. He extended the gun in front of him and slowly began to move it from side to side, trying to get the feel of the dummy, and then when he felt zoned in, he squeezed off three shots more, rapid fire, and the forehead of the silhouette lit up with three flashing lights, each within an inch of another.

"Quite good," the baron said. "The Magnum must be your weapon."

His voice sounded muffled and Remo turned. Standing behind him, alongside the baron, was Namu. In his hand, he held a tray of doughnuts and the baron was busy stuffing one into his mouth.

Namu stared at Remo, smirking. Again, unaccountably, Remo hated him.

"Don't you approve of my shooting, Sambo?" he asked.

Namu was silent.

"I'm sorry, Baron," Remo said. "I forgot he doesn't speak until you pull his chain."

He turned again to the target and picked up the Police special, flipping bullets into it with practiced hands. "This is in your honor, Namu," he said, and emptied six shots, rapid fire. All hit into the groin of the dummy.

He placed the gun down and turned. Namu stood there, still silent, but his eyes glowered with hatred.

"Very, very good, Mr. Kenny," Nemeroff said.

"Sorry, Baron," Remo said. "These are not my weapons."

"No? What is?" Nemeroff asked, and Remo wished he knew. He just knew that the guns, for all his apparent proficiency, had not felt right in his hand. Somehow he knew too that a weapon to be used best, must feel as if it were a part of him, not just a tool. The pistols seemed like tools.

Remo walked back into the storeroom, without answering the baron's question. Nemeroff, his mouth still crammed with doughnut, and Namu followed, watching Remo from the doorway as he looked through the racks of knives.

He held them by their handles, then by their tip; he felt their weight in the palm of his hand. He replaced those that did not feel right. Finally, he had selected four. He had done it individually and was surprised to see that all four were almost identical to each other and to the knife he had found in his hotel room.

He walked back outside, brushing past Nemeroff and under the nose of Namu, but he was able to see Namu look questioningly at Nemeroff who paused, then gave a slight nod of his head.

The alley on the far right of the range was smaller than the others, with a target only twenty feet away, and Remo stepped up to the opening, carrying the four knives by their tips in his left hand.

He reached down with his right hand, took a knife, hefted it once in the palm of his hand, and then raising his hand over his head, fired it at the stuffed dummy. It hit into the waist and buried itself up to the hilt.

He threw the second next to the first, and the third next to the second. He held the fourth knife in his left hand, tip downward, looking at the three knives which formed a small triangle at the center of the target dummy. Then with a flash of his hand, he fired the knife underhand, and it buried itself deeply between the other three knives.

"Bravo," cried Nemeroff. But the man who thought he was P.J. Kenny realized something else. Knives were not his natural weapon either.

"It appears your skill with the gun is exceeded only by your skill with the knife," Nemeroff said.

Remo walked down the stall, toward the target.

Behind him, Namu stepped to the firing line, his eyes on Nemeroff, who had sunk back into his chair, munching on the last of the doughnuts. Nemeroff nodded.

Remo reached his hand forward to pull a knife from the dummy, when he heard it. His ears measured the thrust, the direction, the speed and the force; he froze and the knife flashed through his open fingers, impaling itself deep into the dummy, next to the knife Remo had reached for.

He turned. Namu stood twenty feet away, three knives in his left hand. Remo looked quizzically toward Nemeroff, who said; "Namu is proud of his prowess with the knife. He feels his reputation threatened by your prowess."

"He can have his reputation. The knife is not my weapon," Remo said.

Namu spoke. "Perhaps, Master, the problem is not in the weapons but in the heart." The big man was poised on the balls of his feet, waiting, Remo knew for a word from Nemeroff.

"Explain yourself, Namu," Nemeroff said.

"Cowardice," Namu said. "It is cowardice that makes Mr. Kenny reluctant to decide on weapons. I have heard from the Black Panthers in the city that all white Americans are cowards, who can kill only with armies."

Remo laughed aloud. Nemeroff looked at him, a grin on his horse face. Namu spoke again. "Let me test him, master."

Nemeroff watched Remo's face for emotion, but there was none. He looked at Namu and saw only blind, unreasoning hatred. "You forget yourself, Namu," Nemeroff said. "Mr. Kenny is not only our guest, he is our partner."

"That's all right, Baron," Remo said. "If he was trained by the Panthers, I've got nothing to worry about."

"As you wish," Nemeroff said. He nodded to Namu. The big man turned again toward Remo and lifted a knife into his right hand.

"Wait, Namu," Nemeroff called. "Mr. Kenny must pick his weapons."

"I have my weapons," Remo said.

"Where?"

"My hands," Remo answered, and he knew the answer was right.

Not guns, not knives, just hands.

"Hands against Namu?" Nemeroff was incredulous.

Remo ignored him. "Let's go, Rastus. I've got a date in town."

"With the English trollop?" Namu said, raising the first knife slowly over his head. "It is only by chance that she is still alive."

He fired the first knife. It flashed at Remo, a silver streak, but Remo slowly swayed his body, and the knife passed harmlessly over his shoulder. He smiled, and took two steps toward Namu.

"Maybe the range was too far," Remo said. "Try again. By the way, did your Panther friends tell you the only way you can hurt a white man is to kick him in the shins?"

"Swine," Namu called, and the second knife was on its way toward Remo. Remo was advancing now, moving forward toward Namu, and the knife again missed. Confusion masked the black's face. One knife left in his hand.

He raised it again over his head. Remo moved closer. Twelve feet, then ten, then eight. Then Namu fired. The knife turned one lazy circle in air. But it was doomed to miss too. It went by Remo, alongside his waist, and then his hands flashed in air and the knife stopped, and Remo held it by its handle.

Remo looked at the knife as if it were an insect he had plucked from the air. He took another step toward Namu. "If you were a man," he said, "I'd put this knife where it would hurt."

He tossed the knife to the floor. It hit the wooden boards with a dull thump.

"You're the one who fired the shot at me, aren't you?" Remo asked. He was only five feet from Namu now.

"I fired at the girl. I was unlucky. I killed neither of you," Namu snarled and then with a roar, he lunged at Remo. His giant arms encircled the top of Remo's body, and then Remo, with a laugh, slid out from between his arms and was standing alongside Namu. He put a thumb knuckle into Namu's temple, and the big man fell to the floor.

He was up instantly, wheeling, again advancing on Remo. Remo saw he was coming slower now. He waited until he was up close, and then put a shoe tip in Namu's left knee. He felt jelly under the leather of his shoe. Namu fell again. This time, he screamed, but the scream changed into a shriek: "Imperialist, fascist swine."

He lunged one more time toward Remo, but then went past him scurrying along the counters along the pistol alleys, trying to reach the Magnum and the Police Special that Remo had left at the end. He was too slow.

He arrived at the same time as Remo, and then the ammunition drawer was opened, Namu's hamlike hands were thrust into it, and Remo slammed the drawer shut on Namu's wrists. He could hear the bones crack, and Namu slumped. Remo carefully picked up the Magnum, and fired the remaining shots into the drawer, through the thin wooden partition. The second shot hit bullets and was followed by a string of sharp cracks, Namu shrieked with pain, and then fell to the floor, his hands slowly sliding out of the drawer, the fingers missing, the hands only bloody stumps.

Remo watched him drop, then dropped the empty Magnum onto his chest. "That's the biz, sweetheart," he said.

He walked toward the baron. "You shouldn't let your men go to Panther meetings," he said.

Nemeroff jumped off his seat in unabashed glee. He had never seen such a spectacle. He was pleased; P.J. Kenny was just the man he needed to work with him. And he worked with his hands. No wonder his name was feared in the United States.

Nemeroff pumped his hands in congratulation. Remo noted that he did not even look at the fallen Namu, whose life was fast leaving his body. Just another piece of flesh to Nemeroff, Remo thought. That's worth remembering.

Remo said, "Now you said that there was a little housekeeping chore for me?"

"Yes," Nemeroff said.

"Who is it?"

"There are two men. From America. We have learned of them from our New York contacts. One is a white man; the other an Oriental."

"What are their names?" Remo asked.

"The white man is named Remo Williams. The Oriental is aged. His name is Chiun."

"And you want me to…"

"Exactly. To kill them. It will be child's play for P.J. Kenny."

CHAPTER FOURTEEN

IT WAS NIGHT WHEN REMO headed back to Algiers in the new Porsche convertible the baron had given him. He drove slowly, reflecting on his newly-discovered status as professional killer.

Strange thing: to go to sleep, to wake up knowing nothing, and then to find out that you're an assassin. Oh well, a thing worth doing is worth doing right. He was apparently a good assassin and that was worth something.

He had slowed down to stop at the gate, but two new guards had waved him through, apparently on telephone orders from Nemeroff. And then he was back on the main road, heading for the city, the stars twinkling overhead in a sky that was cold black. He thought of his first assignment.

Remo Williams and Chiun. It was silly, he thought. What did he know about killing? Williams and Chiun might be tough customers. On the other hand, he had done pretty well with Namu. Perhaps some unremembered, but not forgotten, instinct would carry him through where conscious knowledge failed.

Of course, on the other hand, the amnesia would probably begin to lift in the next day or so. Remo Williams and Chiun had not arrived in Algiers yet. By the time they had, P.J. Kenny might be in full control of his skill and experience. He smiled to himself. If that was the case, America would have two dead agents.

Agents. Then he thought of Maggie Waters. She was an agent, too, but of the British. The shot that had wounded him had been meant for her. A flicker of memory passed into his mind. He had seen that big black arm that belonged to Namu holding the machine gun in the back of the car, when the shots were fired at them. That was why Namu had put him on edge. Well, he would put no one on edge any more. Tough luck. He should have had better sense than to listen to the Black Panthers.

He parked his auto in front of the Stonewall Hotel, leaving it unlocked, and walked up the few steps toward the front door of the hotel. He heard a whistle behind him, and turned.

A uniformed policeman stood there, beckoning him with a crooked index finger. Remo stood his ground.

"What do you want?" he asked.

"That car. Whose is it?" the policeman asked.

"Baron Nemeroff's," Remo said. "Anything wrong?"

"No, sir," the policeman said quickly. "Very good, sir. I just wanted to know."

"Keep an eye on it for me," Remo said, turning away, not waiting for an answer, but hearing the policeman's "certainly" over his shoulder.

Nemeroff's name had muscle in Algiers; that was apparent.

Inside, the lobby of the Stonewall looked as if it had been taken over by a convention of *Unione Siciliano*. There was a line of men in blue suits, stringing toward the front desk, waiting to register. They spoke to each other with elaborate gestures and obvious courtesy. At their sides, stood other men, wearing lighter colored suits, and the guns under their left armpits were advertisements for their trade, which was killing.

And all around the lobby, leaning against walls, sitting in chairs pretending to read newspapers, were more men, all of whom looked as if they needed shaves, and it seemed as if their major assignment was to watch one another, judging from the evil glances they threw toward each other.

Their eyes turned to Remo as he entered the lobby, and he moved through the crowd of them toward the elevators.

"Keep up the good work," he told one who snarled at him.

"Good going. You're getting meaner-looking every day," he told another.

"If I didn't know you were here, I'd never have noticed you." And to another, "Seen anything of Mack Bolan around?"

Someone should know P.J. Kenny, he thought. But no one answered him; there was no glimmer of recognition on any face. As the elevator door closed behind him, he saw two steamer trunks in front of the main desk. From behind it, he could see only two robed arms waving wildly through the air. The door closed before his curiosity had a chance to awaken.

Going up, he remembered: it was the face. None of the men in the lobby had ever seen P.J. Kenny. Not the one wearing this face.

The lock had been changed on his door and his key did not work, so he knocked, hoping Maggie was still there.

He heard a click that he recognized as a phone hanging up and movement, and then her clipped voice asking: "Who is it?"

"P.J.," he said.

"Oh, good."

She quickly unsnapped the lock on the door and pulled it back, Remo stepped into the room. She pushed the door closed behind him, then threw her arms about him. She wore a filmy gold negligee that left nothing to his imagination. Her body was as naked as naked and even sexier, and her arms around his neck warmed him. He reached down and pulled her close against him with both hands. She whispered in his ear, hotly, "I was worried. I thought I might never see you again."

"It'd take camels to drive me away from you."

"Bactrian or dromedary?" she asked.

"What's the difference?" he said.

"One hump or two humps."

"I thought you'd never ask," he said.

She stood back from him, her hands on his shoulders, and measured him with her eyes. "You don't look any the worse for wear," she said.

"Neither do you."

"You just can't keep me in the dark," she said "Have you found out who you are?"

"Yes. I'm P.J. Kenny."

"And who is P.J. Kenny?"

"I'm still trying to find out," he lied. "But whatever it is, I think it's bad news."

"You couldn't be bad news," she said.

"Are you trying to seduce me with your kindness?" he asked.

"Seduction is for sissies," she said. "I thought you he-men from America preferred rape."

"Have it your own way," he said as his lips muffled her attempt to say "I will." Then he was pulling off her flimsy gown and walking her backward to the bed.

He carefully arranged her on the bed, but then stood up and slowly began to undress.

"Are you trying to torture me?" she asked.

"Eat your heart out."

"Only as a last resort," she said. Then her hands were helping his him with his clothes, fondling zippers, caressing buttons, then she did the same thing with his flesh under the clothing, then the two were naked on top of the red satin coverlet and they melted together in a confluence of arms and lips and legs.

If he hadn't known better, the man who thought he was P.J. Kenny would have sworn that he had spent the last ten years in a monastery, building up his strength for this encounter.

He was insatiable, unstoppable, undrainable. Every time Maggie tried to talk to him about Nemeroff, he stopped her with sex, and she finally gave up the effort and surrendered to him totally. He took her hour after hour computerishly calculating the effects of his movements on her body. She could only escape her own frenzied lust when she fell into an exhausted sleep at three o'clock in the morning.

Remo slept too.

He slept until eight a.m., when the telephone next to the bed rang softly.

Who the hell would that be? He picked up the phone and growled, "Yeah?"

"This is the bell captain," a heavily accented voice said. "I was told to tell you when someone arrived."

"Who?" Remo asked.

"An old Chinaman. Named Chiun. He registered last night. His room is on your floor. Room 2527."

"Anybody register with him?"

"No. He was alone."

"Anybody register named Williams?"

There was a pause, then: "No. And there are no reservations in that name."

"Room 2527, you say?"

"Yes."

"Thanks."

Remo hung up. So that's what being a professional killer was like. Getting awakened at all hours of the morning. Next to him, Maggie slept on, and as he watched her, he felt lustful again. He reached a hand out and placed it on her left breast, slowly trailing his fingers over the pink-tipped mound, softly and delicately so as not to wake her.

She smiled in her sleep, and her lips opened, then her teeth came down on her lower lip, sparkling white teeth. There was a sudden intake of breath and her body shook, then she sighed and her limbs relaxed, her teeth slid off her lower lip and she smiled again. Remo smiled to himself. Post-hypnotic orgasm. Maybe he could bottle it. The women of the world would find it irresistible. He'd liberate them all from the evil necessity of needing men's bodies. What the battery-operated vibrator had started, P.J. Kenny could finish. Onward and upward. Liberation. Freedom now.

He would have to look into it.

But first, this Chiun.

He slipped out of bed, showered and dressed in slacks, tennis shoes and a blue short-sleeved shirt. He looked at Maggie, still smiling, sleeping in the bed, and then slipped out the door. He got his bearings and headed for Room 2527.

This Chiun was probably a Sumo wrestler. Well, that didn't phase him. After Namu, nothing would.

He stopped outside Room 2527, listening. Inside there was a faint buzzing sound. He listened again. It was someone humming. He reached out and touched the doorknob and slowly turned it. It was unlocked, and he turned the knob all the way, then pushed the door open slowly.

He stood in the doorway, looked into the room and smiled.

Kneeling on the carpet, next to the bed, his back to Remo, was a tiny wisp of an Oriental. Even from the back, the man who thought he was P.J. Kenny could see he was aged and delicate. He could not have weighed a hundred pounds, and more likely, his weight matched his age which Remo would put at eighty.

The old man knelt there, his head lifted, eyes apparently fixed on a window of the room, his hands folded in his lap, and Remo stepped inside the room and softly closed the door. The chink probably hadn't heard him enter. He slammed the door shut. But there was still no movement from the chink, no sign that he had heard. If it were not for the humming, a tuneless chanting sound, Remo would have thought he was dead. But he wasn't dead. Deaf. That was it. The old man was deaf.

Remo spoke.

"Chiun," he said.

The old man rose to his feet, in one smooth motion, and turned to face the man at the door. The parchment face creased into a small smile.

And the man at the door said: "Where's Remo Williams?"

The room must be electrified for sound so he cannot speak, Chiun thought. He shrugged.

"Don't give me that, chink. Where's Williams?"

Remo did not speak that way to Chiun even in jest, and Chiun said: "You speak that way to the Master of Sinanju?"

"Sinanju? What is that? A suburb of Hong Kong?"

Chiun looked hard at the man who had Shiva's face and Shiva's vibrations but was strangely unlike Shiva, and he thought to speak in anger, then he thought to remain silent. He would wait.

The man at the door took another step into the room. He was balanced on the balls of his feet and his hands had risen slightly toward his hips. It was the prelude to attack, and Chiun did not want him to attack.

He had come to love the destroyer he had created; he had come to a grudging respect for the country which paid his wages.

But he was the Master of Sinanju, and a village depended upon his life. He loved Remo, but if Remo attacked, Remo would die. And in that secret part of his heart, where he kept a love he never spoke, Chiun would die too. And he knew that never again would he create a destroyer.

The man who thought he was P.J. Kenny sized up the old man. His brain told him to move in, to throw one blow, and it would all be over. He was too big, too young, too strong. His brain told him that.

But his instinct told him something else. It called something from deep inside his memory and he remembered a voice once telling him that "one should consider the bamboo. It is neither thick nor sturdy. Yet, when come the winds that fell the trees, the bamboo laughs and survives."

This old man in front of him was the bamboo. He could feel the vibrations; they were strong and strange, and he knew the old man felt them too, that those vibrations would add up to a fight that P.J. Kenny would never forget. If he survived it.

He rocked up onto his toes. Then he heard a sound behind him, and he wheeled and faced the door, somehow totally unconcerned about any need to protect his back against the old man. The door pushed open and Maggie stepped in.

She was wearing a light blue dress with nothing under it, and Remo took her by the shoulder.

"I thought I told you to wait."

"I was worried," she said.

"There's nothing to worry about. Now go back to the room." He moved to usher her out and he felt her small shoulder bag slap against her leg. There was more weight in it than there should be; he gauged the weight as just about the right amount for a .32 caliber automatic.

He marched her out into the hall and called over his shoulder, "You wait here, mister." Remo walked Maggie back to the room and pushed her inside roughly. "Now you wait here, this time," he said, and his voice allowed no appeal.

He slammed the door angrily behind him and started back down the hall to Room 2527. He wondered if the chink would still be there, and somehow he knew the chink would be there.

He was there, standing still as a statue, waiting, the wisp of smile playing around his mouth. Remo closed the door behind him and suddenly was moved by pity for the old man. He was so old.

"All right, old man, you're coming with me," Remo said.

"And where are we going?"

"That's none of your business. But when your friend Williams finds out, he'll come after you. And then I've got you both."

"You have always been a master of logic," the old man said. He smiled, remembering that beautiful passage in the Western Bible where God orders Abraham to kill his son.

Chiun was not Abraham; he would not have refused. He was glad that the Gods had heard his prayers and that he would not have to kill Remo.

CHAPTER FIFTEEN

IN THE LOBBY, REMO STEERED Chiun through the phalanxes of gunmen and bodyguards, who looked at the unlikely pair with curious eyes.

Since last night, some of them had obviously gotten word that P.J. Kenny was in the hotel and some surmised that this dude in the tennis shoes might be him, because they took great pains to avert their eyes and look elsewhere when Remo and Chiun passed.

The old man allowed himself to be led quietly outside, which was good for him, Remo told himself. Remo got behind the wheel of the Porsche and began driving off toward the edge of the city and the road that twisted up to Nemeroff's castle.

Next to him, Chiun chuckled.

"What's so funny, old man?"

"It is a lovely day for a drive. I thought we might go to the zoo."

"If you think this is a pleasure trip, you're in for a surprise," Remo said. "As soon as Williams comes for you, *zzzzt*! The two of you get it."

"What have we done to deserve such a fate at your hands?" Chiun asked.

"Nothing personal, old man. My boss, Baron Nemeroff, says you go, so you go. That's it."

"And of course, like a good assassin, you must do your duty?" Chiun asked.

"Of course."

"Good," said Chiun. "I believe you have more character than Remo Williams. He is always letting sentiment interfere with his work."

"That's too bad for him," said the man who thought he was P.J. Kenny. "There's no room for sentiment in this business."

"How true. How true. And what weapons have you reserved for our demise?"

"I haven't decided yet," Remo said. "Generally, I work with my hands."

"Very pure," Chiun said. "Purity is the essence of the art. I never liked this Remo Williams anyway. May I give you a hint as to his weakness?"

"Hint away," Remo said.

"Hit him in his gross American mouth."

"Can't take it in the face, huh?" Remo said.

"Probably his mouth will be filled with all kinds of forbidden foods. Sweetnesses and alcohols and meats with blood."

"Nothing wrong with those things," Remo said. "What else would he eat?"

"Why not rice? Why not fish?" Chiun asked.

"Hey," Remo said. "I had that last night for dinner. It wasn't very good. I don't even know why I ordered it."

"You would think so, my son," Chiun said in disgust. "Tell me of the assassin's life. Is it rewarding? Why do you do it?"

"I do it for the money. It's just a job."

"I see. And the money? Is it adequate?"

"It's more than adequate," Remo said. "I'm a rich man."

"I am sure you are," Chiun said. "Rich, not only in possessions but in purity of spirit. Your mother must be proud of you."

"I think you're on the snot, old man, for some reason I don't know," Remo said. "So why don't you just zipper your face."

"I am sorry, my son. It must be my nerves, stretched to the breaking point in terror at the thought of death at the hands of the one and only P.J. Kenny." Chiun cackled like a chicken, in high good humor.

"Shut up a minute, will you?" Remo said. "We're being tailed." He kept his eyes on the rearview mirror as he moved into the outskirts of the city, varying his speed. Sure. There was a black Jaguar on his tail, keeping up with him, sometimes right behind him, sometimes letting a car or two slide between them. He made a left turn and slowed. Seconds later, the Jaguar made the same left turn and dodged into a parking spot to hide, but the driver had gotten close enough to be seen.

It was Maggie.

"Now what the hell's she doing following us?" Remo said.

"Perhaps she heard you were going to give a demonstration of your killing prowess," Chiun suggested sweetly. "The whole countryside may come to watch you dispatch me and my poor friend, Remo."

"I'll give them their money's worth," Remo said.

"A noble ambition, my son. One I have attempted to follow all my life."

"Three cheers and a tiger for you. I always knew you Chinamen were smart."

"I am a Korean," Chiun informed him, haughtily.

"Same thing," Remo said. "Kissing cousins anyway."

"To have a Chinese for a cousin would make the strongest stomach ill. To kiss one would be beyond revulsion."

"Well, that's your hangup," Remo said. "I always kind of dug their women."

"Yes," Chiun said. "You would."

Remo tooled the car, crisscrossing, in and out of the narrow streets of the old Mustapha quarter of the city, until he was sure that he had lost the Jaguar.

Nemeroff had told him the girl was a British agent, but he had not told him to kill her. And until that word came, the man who thought he was P.J. Kenny wanted to keep Maggie alive, for personal reasons.

He glanced in the mirror again as the Porsche whizzed up the hillside, heading out of the city. The road behind him was clear, so he tromped on the gas pedal and headed for Nemeroff's castle. Today was the big day. The top-level meeting of gangland with Nemeroff. The announcement that he would be the man running the show in Scambia. He wanted to be there for that.

At the castle, Nemeroff was bidding goodbye to a visitor.

He stood on the roof, under the gently revolving blades of a helicopter and clasped Vice President Asiphar's hand in both of his.

"I trust you have enjoyed your visit, my vice president," he said.

Asiphar's black face broke into a broad grin. "Very enjoyable, Baron."

"I know that your pleasure was shared by your companions."

"They will not forget me," Asiphar said.

Nemeroff privately agreed. The two girls Asiphar had used would remember him forever. They would remember him on their trip into total drug addiction, and they would remember him as they were pressed into service in the cheapest of brothels. Perhaps — sometime — they would question their memories and ask if it had happened: if they had really stayed in a castle; if they had been mistresses of a man who became president of a country. But when they mentioned it, they would be laughed at and they would one day stop mentioning it. But they would always remember it. So would Nemeroff; he had television tapes of their performance.

He thought these things as he wished Asiphar Godspeed.

"Return to the palace now," he said. "And await our arrival. Within forty-eight hours, you shall be president. Within forty-eight hours, the world will know your name and begin to feel your power."

Asiphar smiled again, noontime teeth in a midnight face and then clambered heavily up the steps to the helicopter's front seat, the plane rocking as he climbed aboard, and strapped himself in for the ten-minute flight back to Scambia.

———

The helicopter was vanishing in the distance when Remo drove up the dirt road, leading to Nemeroff's castle.

The guards at the sentry post stepped in front of his car, and it skidded to a stop. The guards aimed their rifles at Remo and dogs chained to the sentry boxes began to snarl and pull at their bonds, to get at the car.

Remo rolled down his window and said to the nearest guard:

"Come on, for Christ's sake, you know the car."

"I know the car," the guard said, "but I don't know you. What's your name?"

"P.J. Kenny."

"And the old geezer?"

"My prisoner."

The guard went back into the sentry box and picked up a telephone. While he called, Remo looked at the dogs. They had stopped snarling, and their snouts were lifted in the air. They sniffed the air, delicately, questioningly. Then they both lay down quietly, shivering, whimpering.

"What happened to the dogs, I wonder?" Remo said to Chiun.

"They know the hour of the cat is near," Chiun said softly.

"The hour of the cat? And who is the cat?" Remo asked.

Chiun turned slowly and met his eyes, and then he smiled. "You will soon find out," he said.

The guard replaced the phone and came back to Remo's side of the car. "All right, Kenny. You can go through. The baron's expecting you."

"Thanks for nothing," Remo said.

"Hey," the guard said, "what the hell'd you do to spook these dogs?"

Remo said: "It's almost the hour of the cat. Didn't you know?"

The guard said, "If there's any cat around here, they'll tear it apart and you better believe it."

Then Remo was gone, his car scratching gravel behind him. In the rearview mirror, he saw the guards follow him with their eyes, and the dogs lying still, still cowering, frightened.

Remo pulled into the broad veranda area that served as Nemeroff's parking lot. Already half a dozen cars were there, all black Mercedes limousines identical to the one Namu had first picked up Remo in. The baron's visitors had started to arrive.

Remo left the car in front of the steps, got out, and motioned Chiun to follow. The old man slipped out of the car and slowly followed Remo up the broad stone stairs, his feet under his brocaded blue robe, shuffling softly on the steps.

Nemeroff was seated on the edge of the patio, eating, alone and he waved at Remo who nodded.

"Will you join me at breakfast?" he asked.

"No thanks."

"Who is this man?"

"This is one of the men you wanted. Chiun."

"I wanted him dead," Nemeroff said, chewing on the end of a cinnamon roll.

Remo nodded. "He's as good as dead whenever you want him dead. But I brought him here to try to get his partner, this Williams, to follow. He must be hiding somewhere. There's no sign of him yet."

Nemeroff considered this as he chewed. Before he spoke, he was interrupted by the ring of the telephone at his side.

"Yes," he said.

"I see. All right."

He hung up the telephone and turned a smile on Remo.

"Already, your plan has borne fruit. The guards have captured an agent on the grounds."

"Good," Remo said. "Maybe it's Williams." He turned to Chiun. "Still think it's going to be the hour of the cat, old man?"

Chiun said softly, "The cat has not yet unsheathed its claws."

Nemeroff clapped his hands and a ferret-faced man in a white suit appeared on the balcony.

"Accompany Mr. Kenny as he brings this man to our...visitors' quarters," he said. The man smiled and said, "Yes, sir."

"And prepare for other guests," Nemeroff added.

The guard turned into the building and Remo grabbed Chiun's arm, following him through the study, into the hallway, past the hidden elevator and to a flight of steps in the back of the building.

The steps were damp and musty; the walls were stone and they sweated. The steps zigzagged back and forth, through four landings, until they were in a dungeon deep underground, below the level of Nemeroff's armory.

The steps opened into a narrow passageway, bordered oil each side by heavy wooden doors that had heavy steel locks. The doors were open; the cells stood empty. There were no windows and the only illumination came from bare overhead light bulbs, glittering yellow in the musky air.

"Am I to stay here?" asked Chiun.

"Afraid so, old man," Remo said.

"I will catch my death of cold."

"You'll be gone before the first sniffle," Remo said. "I promise."

"You are always thoughtful."

The guard led them down the dank passageway, the moisture on the stone floor muffling their steps. He stood aside to let Chiun pass, then placed a hand on the old man's shoulder to push him into the last cell on the right.

The guard pushed, but nothing happened. It was as if he had leaned against a wall. He pushed again. Chiun turned toward him.

"Restrain your hands, ferret-faced one," he said.

"Abuse I take from the fearsome P.J. Kenny, but you take no such liberties."

He turned his back then on the surprised guard and stepped into the cell. It held a narrow wooden cot with a limp, springless mattress. There was a sink and a toilet.

"All the comforts of home," Remo said, standing in the door.

"Thank you," said Chiun. "I will remember you with fondness."

"Now why don't you try telling me where Williams is?"

"He is near," Chiun said. "He is near."

Remo heard footsteps coming down the corridor toward them and turned. Along the passageway came Nemeroff, pushing Maggie Waters along in front of him, towering over her in the dim light of the dungeon like some powerful monster from a dream.

He pushed Maggie with one last thrust and she fell against Remo.

"You look surprised, Mr. Kenny," Nemeroff said. "She is the agent that was captured on the grounds."

"I didn't think she had followed me," he said. To Maggie, he said: "A British agent? And I thought you just wanted me for my body." She refused to look up and buried her head against her blue short dress.

Maggie did something very unagentlike. She began to weep.

Nemeroff pushed her again, this time into the reach of the guard. "Put her in a cell," he said, "and make her comfortable." The guard smirked.

He pushed Maggie in the cell opposite Chiun's. She staggered to the middle of the floor, then stood there quietly. Slowly, she lifted her head until she was standing proudly erect.

"Attagirl, kid. Keep a stiff upper lip," Remo called.

She turned to him with a look of total hatred. The guard meanwhile had taken manacles down from a hook on the wall. He snapped a pair on her wrists, and then another pair around her ankles.

All the while, he talked, a soliloquy to himself.

"The little lady's going to like this. Englishwomen always like to show off. The little lady's going to get a chance. To show off everything. Will the little lady like that?"

He kept talking as he took from the same wall hook, a short length of chain with a padlock hung open on its end. "Wait till the little lady sees what I've got planned for her. The little lady's going to be proud to show off the merchandise, isn't she?"

He grabbed the cuffs around Maggie's wrists and pulled her toward the back wall of the cell. Imbedded in the stone floor was a large iron ring, and the guard pressed Maggie's upper body downward, until her wrists were near the ring. Then he looped the chain through the wrist manacles, under the ring, through the chains on Maggie's ankles, and fastened it with the padlock.

"Does little lady like that?" he said. Maggie was facing the rear wall now, bent over from the waist as if trying to touch her toes during her morning exercises. Her short skirt had ridden up over her buttocks, and she wore no undergarments, and Remo could almost sense her embarrassment at the view her jutting posterior gave to the men behind her.

The guard still talked. "Little lady going to be nice to her friends, isn't she?" and he rubbed his hand down one soft buttock.

Nemeroff turned to Remo. "You have enjoyed her. Perhaps I shall give my men that same opportunity before she is sent to her death." He turned again to look at Maggie. "An inviting target, is it not?"

The man who thought he was P.J. Kenny grinned. "I've scored some bulls-eyes on that range," he said.

"And now our Chinese friend," Nemeroff said, turning toward Chiun who still stood motionless in the center of the cell. "Bind him also," he told Remo.

Remo approached Chiun and led him to the ring in the back of the cell. The old man did not resist, and he showed no interest when Remo pulled down the manacles and chains from the wall. Instead, Remo could heard him talking under his breath.

The old man was praying. Remo grinned. He'd finally come to his senses and realized he was going to die, and now he was making peace with his ancestors. Well, good for the little chink, Remo thought, as he fastened the chains and locks.

And then he listened to the old man's words. They were soft and intended for the heavens alone.

"Oh, Masters of Sinanju who have trod this earth before, forgive me my patience with these butchers and animals. Close your eyes to my display of inaction, and consider instead that I suffer their insults so that I may yet save the one who will be the next Master of Sinanju.

"But my patience even now grows thin and the hour of the cat is near at hand. Guide my wisdom, as my experience will guide my hand."

"Say one for me, too," Remo said, as he stood up from fastening the last chain. Then he strutted from the cell into the passageway where Nemeroff and the guard waited.

To the guard, Nemeroff said, "You watch these two."

To Remo, he said, "You can dispose of them at your leisure later, but now you must come with me."

"I saw that your guests are arriving," Remo said, as he followed Nemeroff down the passageway.

"Yes," Nemeroff said. "Our meeting will begin soon. But we have another visitor. One of our New York operatives has arrived. He has seen this Remo Williams. Perhaps he may be of help to you in capturing him."

"Maybe," Remo said. "Who is this guy?"

"His name is O'Brien," Nemeroff said. "He is a guard at the New York federal prison. He has done invaluable service to us there."

"Good," Remo said. "I can't wait to meet him."

CHAPTER SIXTEEN

REMO FOLLOWED NEMEROFF UP THE steep flights of damp stone stairs to the first floor.

As they stood momentarily in the large entrance hall, Nemeroff walked away from him.

"Mr. Fabio. How are you? So happy you could come."

An olive-skinned man had just walked through the glass doors from the first floor patio. He looked up at Nemeroff with the Mafia's traditional look — halfway between cowardice and toleration — which passed for respect, and stiffly stuck out his hand.

"Who's that?" he asked Nemeroff, gesturing with his head over the baron's shoulder toward Remo.

The baron laughed. It was that evil whinny of a laugh that greeted things he thought were funny.

"Oh, yes," he said, still braying. "I want the two of you to meet."

He took his visitor by the elbow and led him toward Remo. Outside, Remo could see Fabio's bodyguard lounging on a chair on the patio, trying to appear unconcerned, but watching the activities through the glass, ready to move if it became necessary. He was exiled to the patio because it was considered bad form to bring one's bodyguard into another man's home.

Then Remo had his hand stuck into the hand of Fabio.

He looked hard at the face and knew he should have known it, but it was just another wop with the brains of an organ-grinder. Who he was just wasn't worth the effort.

He heard Nemeroff say: "This is Mr. Fabio. He is an important man in the United States."

Remo looked harder at him. The man had a fleshy face, and a small thin scar ran from the corner of his left eye to the bottom of his left ear. The skin was whiter than his normal skin, he had splashed powder on his face to try to equalize the color but he was still scarred and hideous.

And then Remo heard Nemeroff say:

"And this is my associate, Mr. P.J. Kenny."

Fabio's hand tensed in his and then removed itself, not recoiling suddenly as if from fear, but moving back deliberately as if for a reconsideration, and then he heard Fabio speak:

"Dat ain't P.J. Kenny."

Nemeroff whinnied again, so Remo adopted his mood and smiled as Nemeroff said:

"Good. That is proof of how successful the plastic surgery was."

Remo watched as Fabio's little pig eyes burned into his. Then Fabio said:

"P.J., is it really you?"

Remo nodded. Fabio stared a little longer. Then his pig features relaxed into a smile. He took a step forward, raised his right hand, palm up, to signify surprise, and then brought his hand around Remo's shoulders in a half bear hug.

"P.J.," he said. "I've been wondering what happened to you. Everybody was."

"I was under the knife for the new face," Remo said, hoping that was the right thing to say. "And then the baron arranged for me to come here and join him."

"And join him," Fabio mimicked. "Maybe that doctor operated on your brain, too. You talk better than you used to."

"Thanks," said the man who thought he was P.J. Kenny. "Part of my new image."

"I'll tell you, your new image is a lot better than your old image," Fabio said. "You was about the ugliest-looking thing I ever saw."

"Wasn't I, though? I looked downright Italian," Remo said. When

Fabio paused, unsure how to answer, Remo added, "and now I look Neapolitan," giving the word the extra Italian accent on the last syllable, guessing that Fabio was Neapolitan because of the way he had raised his hand in greeting.

Fabio laughed out loud. "Yeah," he said, "that's a real improvement. And you're in with the baron?"

"Right-hand man," Remo said.

Nemeroff moved quickly into the conversation.

"Mr. Kenny has agreed to join with all of us in insuring that whatever agreement we reach will be fairly kept. I think he has that reputation for fairness," Nemeroff said.

"You bet he has," Fabio said. "Hey, P.J. — remember when you got my brother, Matty?"

"Sure do," Remo smiled. "It was some job."

"Some job?" Fabio laughed. "They was picking up pieces of him for weeks."

"Yeah," Remo laughed. "I used my special cheese cutting knife for that job." Then he added, "Ho, ho, ho."

"Hee, hee, hee," laughed Fabio, remembering the one hundred twenty-seven pieces of the remains of his brother, Matthew, whose crime had been that he held up to ridicule the son of another gangland leader.

"Ha, ha, ha," whinnied Baron Nemeroff. Then he turned the smile and laugh off as if by a switch, and said,

"Come, Mr. Fabio. We will go to the meeting room upstairs. Some of our mutual friends have already arrived."

He stepped toward the picture on the wall and pressed the button hidden in the molding of the frame. The door slid quietly open.

He stepped aside to allow Fabio to enter first, and turned to Remo: "The man — O'Brien — is in the study. Perhaps he can tell you more about this Williams. What he looks like or what to look for."

Remo nodded and waited until Nemeroff had entered the elevator and pressed the button for the fifth floor. The painting moved softly back over the door opening.

Remo turned and walked across the parquet floor, his tennis shoes noiseless on the highly polished wood. The door was a giant wooden panel, deeply carved with elaborate filigrees, but it pushed open as though it had been hinged on ball bearings.

The room was dark. Remo found himself looking at the stark silhouette of a man, who stared out the first floor window toward the end of the house. Over his shoulder, through the window, Remo could see a red helicopter coming into view. He realized the man was following the helicopter's flight with his eyes. Though neither knew, it was the craft that had taken Vice President Asiphar the few miles to the Scambian Presidential palace where he expected, within forty-eight hours, to occupy the presidential bed.

Remo moved up behind the man, close enough to touch him, and he said, "O'Brien?"

The man wheeled and as he turned, released the heavy drapes he had been holding, and the room again leaked into semi-darkness. But Remo could see the man's face was startled, and the man said: "Boy, you gave me a fright, sneaking up on me like that."

"Tennis shoes," Remo said, as if that explained it. "The baron tells me you know this Remo Williams?"

"No," O'Brien said, "I don't know him. But I saw him once." He brushed past Remo and walked back to a small chair alongside a desk, and plopped down heavily into it.

Remo turned, the sun glistening between the drapes now at his back and shining into O'Brien's face.

"What's he look like?" Remo asked.

"Well, when I saw him, he was dressed like a priest," O'Brien said.

"That's not going to help me much."

"Wait. I'm trying. He had brown eyes, but not like regular brown eyes. They were deep, like they had no black. All deep-colored. You know what I mean?"

"Yeah."

"And he had a hard face. Like he was dressed like a priest, but he sure didn't look like any priest. His nose was straight and he was the kind of guy that looked right in your eye."

O'Brien squinted to try to get a better look at the man standing in front of the window, but all he could see was the outline of his head and body.

"All right," Remo said, "cut the art class lectures. How big was he?"

"He was a big guy, but not that big. Maybe six feet. Not heavy either. But big thick wrists, like he worked on a chain gang or something."

Remo moved closer to O'Brien's chair. O'Brien was casually inspecting his toes. Remo leaned onto the desk top.

"Yeah, go on," he said.

O'Brien looked up, squinting. "As I said, he had thick wrists. Like yours," he added, glancing down at Remo's hands on the desk. "And there was something else."

"What's that?"

"It was his mouth. It like didn't have any lips. It was thin and hard looking and you just knew he was a badass. That was some bad mouth," O'Brien said. He looked up and squinted again into Remo's shadowed face, reflecting slowly, "It was like yours."

"And his eyes were brown?" Remo asked.

"Yeah. Brown…like yours."

"And his hair?"

"It was dark," O'Brien said. "Dark…like yours." He jumped up from the chair and his hand flashed to his side, but then his hand didn't work anymore and he was back in his chair, and a pain more excruciating than any he had ever felt before was happening along his partially-crippled right arm, and the man who thought he was P.J. Kenny said, "What the hell's the matter with you? What are you trying to pull a gun on me for?"

O'Brien said, "Don't give me that. How'd you get here?"

"What are you talking about?" Remo said. "I work for the baron."

"Sure," O'Brien sneered. "He just went ahead and hired Remo Williams."

"Remo Williams? What the hell are you talking about?"

"You're him, man. Maybe you can shit the baron but you can't shit me. You're Remo Williams."

"And you're nuts. I've been assigned to kill Williams."

"Well, just cut your wrists, man," O'Brien said. "And Williams'll die of the bleeding."

"You're dreaming," Remo said.

"Look, Williams," O'Brien said. "I don't know what you're pulling here, but how about letting me in on it? I can probably be some help to you."

Remo was busy trying to sort out what O'Brien had said, but it was all wrapped up in darkness. He was P.J. Kenny. But this man said he wasn't. This man would know and he said that he was Remo Williams. But how could he be?

"I just had plastic surgery," Remo said. "It must just be a coincidence."

"No way," O'Brien said. "How about it? You and me? Fair split?"

A fair split. Remo thought about it for a second, O'Brien's hand went toward his gun again, and Remo suddenly hated this man who had brought confusion into a life that was simplifying into the daily humdrum of the professional assassin. So he reached high into the air and brought the side of his fist down against the top of O'Brien's skull and heard the bones cracking like ice cubes splintering in a warm mix and O'Brien slumped forward in his chair, dead.

Remo let the body fall heavily onto the floor.

Remo Williams? How could it be? He was P.J. Kenny. Nemeroff had known him. Maggie had known him. How could he be Williams?

But there was the chink. Had the chink recognized him when he stepped into that door at the hotel? Had the chink known he was Remo Williams? Then why hadn't he said something? Why had he just stood there, waiting to be killed by P.J. Kenny?

He tried to consider the moves and every move came back to Chiun, to that old Oriental calmly awaiting death in his cell, humiliatingly bound, wrist and ankle to the floor, and Remo knew his answer was there and he would have to confront the old man.

At that moment, the telephone rang. It sat on a small walnut table in the center of the room and Remo stepped over and picked it up. "Hello."

"This is Nemeroff. Was O'Brien any help to you?"

"Yes," Remo said. "A great help."

"Good. May I talk with him, please?"

"Afraid not, baron," Remo said, looking at the body. "He's lying down." He saw the brains and blood oozing from O'Brien's skull. "He said he had a splitting headache."

There was a pause. "Oh, all right," Nemeroff said. "I am just beginning my meeting now. My men will have to forego their pleasure with the Englishwoman. Would you please dispose of her and the Oriental and then join us up here in the fifth floor conference room?"

"Yes, sir. As fast as my little legs can carry me," Remo said.

"Thank you. We will all be waiting."

Remo hung up the telephone, looked at it momentarily, then stepped out into the hall. He would have to confront the old Oriental, and clear up this mystery once and for all.

CHAPTER SEVENTEEN

THE DUNGEON CORRIDOR WAS EMPTY, even though Nemeroff had told ferret-face to watch the prisoners. The mold felt damp and slippery under Remo's feet as he slid down the dungeon corridor to Chiun's cell.

The door was locked, bolted heavily with an iron lock that weighed four pounds. Remo took the lock in his hands, and looked around to call the guard for the key, but then changed his mind for some reason, and twisted the lock in his hands until the metal fractured and it came loose from the door.

He quietly laid the two pieces on the floor, listening. There was no sound in the dungeon except the soft sobbing of Maggie in her cell, behind the closed door, across the narrow passageway. She would be next, but first, the Oriental.

Remo pulled the door open slowly, and remembered how he had last seen the old man, helpless, wrists and ankles chained to the floor.

The door opened softly. The old man sat on the bunk in the cell, a full six feet away from the metal ring, and Remo looked toward the ring.

It was inch-thick steel and it had been sheared in half. Laying next to it were the chains. Broken. So were the ankle and wrist manacles, mashed and broken as if they had been pounded by a hammer wielded with enormous power.

But of course that was impossible, since the old man's hands and feet would have been in the chains when such a hammer was wielded and he would have suffered injury.

The old man stood as Remo walked into the cell, then bowed from the waist and smiled.

For the moment, Remo would not ask how he had escaped. There were other, more important, things for the man who thought he was P.J. Kenny.

"Old man," he said, "I need your help."

"You have but to ask."

"I think I know who I am, but I'm not sure. Help me."

Chiun looked at the small bandage still covering Remo's temple. "You received a blow on the head, did you not?"

"Yes."

"And it was after that that your memory disappeared?"

"Yes."

"Then perhaps a similar blow," Chiun said, and before Remo could move or react, a small rock-hard fist lashed out, and a thumb knuckle hit against his temple, missing the exact mid-point of the bone by a precise 32nd of an inch, and Remo lived by exactly that distance. He saw stars. He shook his head to clear it. And then in a rush of memories, his life flooded back into him: his identity, his mission, who he was and why he was here.

"I know," he said, smiling happily, yet shaking his head from the shock of the attack. "I know. I'm Remo."

"I am glad," Chiun said. "I have something for you." And then, quicker than eye could see or body could move, the old man's hand lashed out, open, fingers extended, thumb drawn in alongside the fleshy part of the palm, and the four extended fingers slapped Remo's cheek with a sharp report.

Remo's head spun, and he growled, "C'mon, Chiun, now what the hell was that about?"

"That is for calling Sinanju a suburb of Hong Kong and for calling me a Chinaman. That is for being insolent to your elders. That is for not staying on your diet and for consorting with women and for bothering Doctor Smith and for endangering your country's interests."

"Had you worried, huh?"

"Worry? About a piece of worthless carrion who will, without me, eat himself to death in a week? What is to worry?"

When he had been P.J. Kenny, Remo had planned to ask how the old man had broken his iron bonds. Now that he was again Remo Williams, the question was not necessary. The old man had broken his bonds because he was Chiun, the Master of Sinanju, and because there had never been anything quite like him in the world before. Even if he felt he was getting old, there was color in his cheeks now and the happiness of the hound on the chase.

"Come, Chiun, we have things to do," Remo said, turning toward the door.

"A common pattern," Chiun said. "First the personal abuse, and now the orders. Do this. Do that. Am I to be treated like a wage slave? Is there no respect due a man my age, a frail old specter barely able to stand erect?"

"Don't," Remo said. "You'll have me in tears. And let me warn you. If you kill anybody this trip, you clean up the bodies yourself."

"You are without feeling, without soul, without heart."

They were both now in the corridor, and could hear Maggie's faint sobbing from behind the closed door of her cell. The door had no lock, and Remo pushed it open softly.

Maggie was there as she had been left. But the dress that had ridden up on her buttocks, was now slung up over her hips. The ferret-faced guard stood behind her, his back toward Remo. His right hand moved rhythmically, back and forth between Maggie's legs, and Remo saw he held a gun in his right hand. He was giggling and still talking to himself. "There's more for the little lady where that came from. Stay with poppa and poppa will give the little lady all she wants."

Remo cleared his throat. The guard partially turned and saw Remo there. Chiun was in the shadow of the corridor and was unseen. The guard grinned at Remo and giggled again. "She likes you, P.J. but she likes this better. Don't you, little lady?" Then his left hand reached over and joined his right between Maggie's legs, working the gun in and out.

Remo spoke, and his voice was edged ice.

"I like your style, kid. You're being promoted."

The guard turned to look at Remo. "Yeah?"

"Yeah. Right upstairs." Then there was a knuckle in the windpipe. It hurt too much to cough and he was dying too fast to choke, so the guard fell onto the damp floor.

"Or downstairs, as the case may be," Remo said.

Maggie glanced over her shoulder, as far as she could in her position, and saw Remo. At first her face showed relief, and then it turned again into a mask of hatred.

Remo moved around in front of her and Chiun joined him, quietly lowering her dress over her flanks.

"You," she said to Remo. "Leave me alone. I don't want any help from you."

"Maggie, honey. I can't explain now, but trust me. We're on the same side."

She started to speak, to spit out her distrust, her hatred, but then Chiun stood alongside Remo and the look in his eyes told her somehow that everything was now all right.

She watched as Chiun and Remo knelt on the floor next to the iron ring. Then they each launched a hand slash at the ring. The two blows landed only a fraction of a second after each other. The vibrations that Chiun started in the metal, Remo interrupted; the metal swallowed its own vibrations, and the inch-thick-ring screeched in pain, then splintered into fragments.

Then, as if the locks were not there, the iron bands on her wrists and ankles were broken, and the chains fell heavily to the floor.

Maggie straightened up, painfully, rubbing her wrists which had been chafed raw by her writhing movements on the point of the guard's gun. She stared disbelievingly at the broken shards of steel on the floor, the remnants of the manacles that had held her so tightly.

Then, Remo had her by the elbow and said, "Come. Nemeroff is waiting for us."

She followed Remo and Chiun out of the cell, then stopped, and went back in. The guard's gun lay at his fingertips. It was a .45 automatic. She picked it up.

"I may need this," she said to Remo.

"Don't get in our way. It'll be safer."

"For whom, Mr. Kenny?" she asked.

"For all of us. And I'm not Mr. Kenny."

They moved quickly up the stairs leading to the main floor, Chiun leading the way. By the time Remo and Maggie had reached the first floor, Chiun was pressing the secret button for the elevator. Remo asked him: "How did you find that?"

"It gives off vibrations. One must listen for them."

"I didn't hear a thing," Remo said.

"Of course not. The perpetually-opened mouth impedes the efficiency of the sometimes-opened ear," Chiun said and led them into the elevator.

Remo pressed the button marked V.

CHAPTER EIGHTEEN

EVERY SEAT AT BARON NEMEROFF'S conference table had been filled.

From all over the world they had come, white men, black men, yellow men. They wore the costumes of their native countries: dashikis from Africa, cotton suits from Asia, dark blue mohair from the United States.

Among them, the thirty-odd men present had accounted for thousands of deaths on a one-by-one basis; they had sent thousands of girls to the brothels; through them, tens of thousands of adults and children had fallen prey to the perils of the needle.

They thought of themselves as indispensable businessmen in an indispensable business. And across all the lines of all their businesses ran the influence of Baron Isaac Nemeroff and when he called, they all came.

Now they all listened.

Overhead, the helicopters flew with their slow flapping sound, occasionally shrouding the room in a flash of shadow as one passed over the multi-colored, glass dome set over the conference table.

Angelo Fabio, the biggest man in the United States was toying with a pencil between his fingertips. Nemeroff's idea seemed to make good sense to him. Occasionally, he would look up and his eyes would meet those of Fiavorante Pubescio who had come from California or Pietro Scubisci who had come from New York, wearing his dirty suit and carrying his omnipresent bag of peppers. He would nod and they would nod in agreement.

Still something nagged at Fabio; he wished he could pinpoint it.

Nemeroff stood at the head of the table, towering over the seated men, his blotchy face flushed with excitement as he spoke to them.

"Consider, gentlemen. Our own nation. Under crime's flag. Where no laws will be enforced that we do not want enforced. Where poppies will grow freely in the fields. Where hunted men from anywhere on the face of the earth can find shelter and refuge."

He looked around the table, from man to man, to murmurs of approvals. One man spoke. He was short and thin; his skin was yellow; his white suit was wrinkle-free; but Dong Hee, crime's undisputed king in the Far East, ran a finger down the crease in his sleeve as he spoke:

"How do we insure this Asiphar's loyalty?"

Nemeroff noted the "we," and with a faint smile turned to the tiny Korean.

"If you will look at the screen up over the elevator door, gentlemen. Behind you, Mr. Hee." Nemeroff leaned forward, pressed a control button imbedded in the wood of the table, causing a plywood section of the wall over the elevator door to slide back revealing a six-foot-square television screen.

Men pushed their chairs back from the table, so they could swing their bodies around and look at the screen.

Nemeroff pressed another button. Immediately, the sound of a voice was heard. "Oh, do it. Do it some more." It was a man's voice, thick and guttural, and it was pleading. Then the screen lightened into a picture of Asiphar, his fat body a study in black against the white sheets, being violated by a fair-skinned blonde girl armed with a hand vibrator. They were naked.

Nemeroff let it run for thirty seconds, then turned down the sound, but let the picture continue.

He cleared his throat and eyes turned back to him.

"That is your soon-to-be-President Asiphar," he said coldly. "He is a swine. He will do anything for the promise of a woman."

Dong Hee spoke again. His English was precise and delicate, as were his features. "That is so, Baron, I am sure. But when he is president, what guarantee will we have that…satisfying his aberrations will still be enough?" As he spoke, his right side and shoulder flickered with the bluish color from the TV screen. "After all, as president, he should be able to make his choice of women. He will have wealth, position. Will he really need us to be his pimps?"

The others had been watching Hee with interest. Now they turned to Nemeroff for his answer.

"You make a very good point, Mr. Hee." As he looked around the room, he saw a puzzled look on Fabio's face. "True enough, as president of Scambia, Asiphar would have certain power. But as for wealth? Whatever his dreams are, they will not be realized.

"For the last five weeks, a crew of workmen has been laying a sewer next to the wall of the east wing of the Scambian presidential palace. They are no ordinary sewer workmen; they are my men.

"When President Dashiti is assassinated, at that very moment, the national treasury of Scambia will be removed from its vaults, in the east wing of the palace. Our Asiphar will find that he is the head of a country without funds even to pay for its president's funeral. He will be on an allowance. From us."

There were murmurs of approval around the table. Hee nodded his head to Nemeroff in satisfaction. Fabio remembered what he wanted to ask:

"What about P.J. Kenny? Why is he here?"

"I was coming to that, Mr. Fabio, because that is another guarantee of Asiphar's cooperation." Nemeroff slowly scanned the table, meeting individually as many pairs of eyes as he could, before speaking again. "Those of you who are from the United States have, I am sure, heard of Mr. P.J. Kenny. Certainly, you have heard of his work. I daresay many of you from other nations have also.

"It is my proposal to keep Mr. Kenny in Scambia as our resident manager, as it were. He will guarantee President Asiphar's cooperation, because Asiphar will be given to understand that if he steps out of line, Mr. Kenny will slit his throat. Mr. Kenny's presence will have another benefit too. I think it would have a dampening effect upon the ambitions of anyone who might try to display his entrepreneurship in Scambia." The words were soft and measured, but the meaning was blunt and hard, even to the Americans who had never heard the word entrepreneur. Anyone who stepped out of line, who tried to get cute and take over the Scambia setup, would be killed. By P.J. Kenny. Who never missed.

"Does that answer your question, Mr. Fabio?"

Fabio grunted.

Nemeroff added, "Mr. Kenny is in the castle right now and I expect him here momentarily. I would like to caution some of you who have seen him in the past that you will not recognize him. He has undergone plastic surgery recently, to facilitate his departure from his own country. He will not look like the man you may remember."

"Just so he works like the man we remember."

"He does," Nemeroff said, smiling at the underboss from Detroit. "In fact, he is awesome. That and his reputation for fairness should make him an ideal representative for us in Scambia."

There were nods of agreement from the Americans, most of whom were clustered around the far end of the long table. Fabio was busy now watching Asiphar on the screen and had forgotten what the discussion was about. All he could think of was that blonde on the screen. She knew some tricks. He wondered if she was in the castle. He would ask Nemeroff before he left.

"What is the financial arrangement to be?" Hee asked.

"I was coming to that. Here, now, we represent twenty-two different countries. From the United States, there are eight major families. For the purpose of this discussion, each family will count as a country. I am asking each of you for $500,000. For your membership in our private country." He smiled, his face breaking in the big horse grin. "And for each man you send, the fee will be $25,000."

"And what do we get out of it?" asked Pubescio from California.

"I am sure, Mr. Pubescio, that you will understand that the $25,000 per person is what is paid to Scambia. In other words, to me, to Mr. Kenny, to President Asiphar. But what you charge for your service is, of course, up to you. I need not point out that $25,000 is a ridiculously inexpensive cost to a man fleeing for his life."

"And what about the $500,000?" Pubescio said.

"That gives you the right to determine who shall be permitted to go from your area to Scambia. I think you quickly see that that power carries with it great monetary value. In just months, you will recover all that sum and much more, I know.

"There are other things which may have crossed your minds also," Nemeroff said. "There will also be ways to send people to Scambia, who might meet with a terrible accident upon running into Mr. Kenny. That could be arranged."

The American leaders looked at each other and smirked. They understood. So did Dong Hee. Soon, so did the others. Around the table heads were nodding.

"Gentlemen, I do not wish to press you for time, but it is of the essence. Within 48 hours, our plan will be underway. I must have your answers now."

"And suppose our answer is no?" Hee asked.

"Then it shall be no. Nothing could be done at this late hour by anyone to thwart our plan. If any of you choose not to participate, that would be your decision. But I would then reserve the right to deal with others in your country, to try to interest them in our proposal."

"It costs too much," Fabio said. That is what he always said at any discussion of any new idea. And then he always went along. Men at the table buzzed, discussing the idea with their neighbors.

Nemeroff had them; he knew it. He had primed Dong Hee well and Hee had handled his role perfectly, firing the questions with just the right degree of animosity, but allowing Nemeroff to calmly break down the resistance that was everyone's natural posture.

Hee stood. "Baron," he said. "It will be a pleasure to join with you."

Nemeroff cocked an ear. He heard the faint whoosh of the elevator.

"Thank you, Mr. Hee. Gentlemen, I believe Mr. Kenny is coming. Perhaps some of you would like to meet our resident manager."

He came from the end of the table and walked toward the elevator door, separated from the main room by a simple mahogany panel.

The elevator door opened and the man known as P.J. Kenny stepped out.

"Mr. Kenny," Nemeroff said. "There are gentlemen here who would like to meet you."

"I've brought company," Remo said. Eyes at the table turned toward the elevator, and strained to get a look at the new arrivals, and Chiun and Maggie stepped out of the elevator after Remo.

"I thought you were going to dispose of them," Nemeroff said.

"You thought wrong," Remo said coldly, stepping from behind the mahogany panel and standing next to Nemeroff, under the television pictures of Asiphar and his woman, casually looking around the conference room, meeting the faces that stared back at him intently.

Nemeroff put a hand on Remo's shoulder and hissed into his ear: "What's wrong with you, Mr. Kenny? The whole plan's ready to go."

"Two mistakes, Baron," Remo said. "First, I'm not P.J. Kenny; I'm Remo Williams. And second, the plan's not ready to go; you are."

He took another step into the room, and Chiun stepped out from behind the mahogany panel. Almost as if by magnetism, his eyes were drawn to those of Dong Hee, who was turned in his seat, casually watching the scene at the elevator door.

He tensed when he saw the old Oriental in the blue robes.

"Who is that man?" he said to Nemeroff.

Nemeroff looked at Chiun, who stepped closer to Hee. "I am the Master of Sinanju," Chiun said.

Hee screamed. The sound unleashed the room into action.

Hee stood and tried to run. Men scrambled to their feet, their hands moving with practiced ease toward guns under their jackets. Chiun seemed to float in the air and then he was atop the conference table. His blue robes flowed around him, angelically, but his face was that of an angel of death and he roared, in a hollow, doom filled voice: "Despoilers of men and jackals of crime, your end is here. It is the hour of the cat."

Hee screamed again. He was still trying to get away from the press of men in chairs, to escape the legend he had heard of all his life, and then his head dropped limply to his side, as a stroke from the old man's hand crushed his neck.

Chiun swirled along the table like a dervish. Men scattered; more drew guns; shots were fired, and through them all, now on the table, then on the floor, raced Chiun, the Master of Sinanju.

Remo took Maggie's arm and pulled her into the room next to him, as he leaned casually against the wall.

"Watch him," he said. "He's really good." He really was, too, Remo thought. Where had he ever gotten the idea that Chiun had grown old?

Chiun moved faster now, faster than bullets, faster than men's hands. Men converged on him and grasped only each other as he was not there, and then his hands and feet were there and bodies hit the floor.

Knives appeared but were wrested from their holders' hands, only to reinsert themselves in their owners' stomachs. Pencils and pens from the table became deadly missiles finding their marks in throats and eyes. One pen hit the mahogany panel next to Remo. It went all the way through the inch-thick hardwood, its point protruding through the other side.

"Hey, Chiun," Remo called, "watch that." To Maggie, he said, "He's good, right? Wait until he warms up." Maggie could only watch in stunned horror. It was like a butcher shop.

Bodies were piled, now. Men no longer fought for the chance to get at the old man. They came now for the door. But between them and the elevator door stood Remo Williams and there began another pile of bodies.

And then there were no more men standing. Only Remo and Chiun and Maggie who surveyed the carnage of the conference room. It looked like a Wall Street version of the St. Valentine's Day massacre.

"Not too good, Chiun," Remo said. "I was watching. You took two strokes on that big goon from Detroit. And you missed the target completely with this pen." He pointed to the pen in the mahogany panel. "You know what a pen like that costs?" he said. "And now it's not even good for writing or anything."

"I am contrite," Chiun said, his hands folded inside the sleeves of his robe.

"Yep," Remo said, "and your elbow was crooked again. Flying up there like Jack Nicklaus on the backswing. How many times do I have to tell you you're never going to amount to anything if you don't keep the elbow close to your side? Can't you learn anything?"

"Please tell me who you are," Maggie suddenly pleaded.

"It's best you don't know," Remo said. "But we're from America. And our assignment was the same as yours. Break this up."

"And you are not P.J. Kenny?"

"No. I killed him before I got here." He interrupted himself as he saw a ghostly flicker in the highly polished wood of the wall across the room. He stepped into the room and looked up over his head. "Hey, look, the movie's on. Let's watch." He watched for a second, and said, "On second thought, Maggie, you better not watch."

He looked around the room. "Now let's see where Nemeroff is."

He walked toward the head of the table and turned a body over with his toe, then looked up, annoyed. "Chiun, is he over there?"

"No," Chiun said.

"Maggie. You got him by you?"

She forced herself to look at the bodies that littered the floor around her. No Nemeroff. She shook her head.

"He escaped, Chiun. He got away," Remo said.

"If you had been more a participant and less an observer, perhaps that might have been prevented," Chiun said.

"There were only thirty, Chiun. I wanted to leave them for you, so I could see what you're going to do with the bodies. Now where the hell did he go?"

There was a hard whirring sound overhead.

"The roof," Remo said. "The helicopters. He's up there." He looked around for panels, for stairways. He saw nothing. He looked up. A helicopter was settling down on the roof, its blades cutting swaths of darkness in the room as they revolved above the glass dome.

"How the hell do we get up there?" Remo asked.

Chiun answered.

First he was on the floor, then on the table, and then he was hurtling through the air, toward the dome, and he hit into it feet first. It crashed. He turned his body in air, grabbed a cross bar with his hands and pulled himself through the opening in the shattered glass.

Some old man, Remo thought.

He followed, springing onto the table and jumping up for a handhold on the cross bar. He hoisted himself through the break in the glass, calling over his shoulder, "Stay there, Maggie."

Then he was on the roof, alongside Chiun. But they were too late for Nemeroff. His red helicopter was already off the roof, and then it dipped its nose and sped off toward the south toward Mozambigree, toward the island nation of Scambia.

CHAPTER NINETEEN

NEMEROFF'S SECOND HELICOPTER WAS taking off at the other end of the roof as Remo and Chiun raced toward it. They reached it just as it started to speed up its rotor, and with dives, they grabbed the right wheel struts.

Above them, the engine roared and lugged, and tried to lift. But their weight unbalanced the craft. It lifted and dropped; lifted again and dropped.

Above their heads, the helicopter window opened. The co-pilot made his first and last mistake. He reached out, and tried to throw a punch at Chiun. Chiun reached up with a toe, then the co-pilot was coming through the window. He hit the stone covered roof and lay in a personal heap.

Remo moved up the struts and slid in through the window. A moment later, the pilot came out the same window. Seconds later, the craft sat down heavily on its haunches and the rotor stopped as Remo cut the engines.

The door opened and Remo jumped out onto the roof. His eyes joined Chiun's in looking forward to the horizon toward which the red helicopter of Baron Nemeroff was speeding.

"Must we pursue?" Chiun said.

"Yes."

"Can you fly this craft?"

"No," Remo said. "Can you?"

"No. But if I were a white man I would be able to use a white man's tools."

They heard behind them the sound of a motor and they turned. As they watched, a section of roof lifted up and then a small screened elevator rose onto their level. In it was Maggie.

As she stepped out, she said: "He had a secret door. I found it. Where is he?"

Remo pointed to the helicopter, now far away in the distance.

"Well, why don't we follow him?"

"I can't fly this damn thing."

"Get in," she said. "I can."

"I always knew there was something about you limey women that I liked," Remo said.

He hopped up into the plane. Maggie clambered up on her side and Chiun slid in alongside Remo, sitting between and behind Maggie and Remo, watching.

"How does this thing fly?" he asked, as Maggie started the engines and they kicked on with a whooshing sound.

He sounded worried.

"C'mon, Chiun, you never saw a helicopter before?" Remo asked.

"I have seen many of them. But I have never been in one and therefore did not examine the problem closely. How does this thing fly without wings?"

"Faith," Remo said. "Blind faith holds it up."

"If body gas from passengers with eating problems would hold it up, we would have no trouble," Chiun said.

Then the craft was off the roof, hovering, and expertly Maggie worked the stick, dipping its nose. Then with a powerful swish, it began moving forward, climbing, gaining speed and altitude, following on the trail of Baron Nemeroff.

"Why must we chase him?" Chiun said. "Why don't we just land somewhere and call Smith?"

"Because if we don't stop him, he'll go through with his plan anyway to assassinate the President. We've got to stop that."

"Why must we always get involved with other people's problems?"

Chiun said. "I think we should sit down somewhere and calmly consider the prospects."

"Chiun, be quiet," Remo said. "You're here now and we're flying to Scambia. We'll be there in just a few minutes so don't worry about it." And to Maggie, he said: "You're pretty good at this. Her Majesty teaches you agents everything."

"Not at all," she shouted over the roar of the blades. "Private lessons."

"Thank heavens for resourceful Englishwomen," Remo said.

"Amen," she said.

"Amen," Chiun said. "Yes. Amen. But keep praying."

Slowly they began to gain on the red helicopter ahead of them. It had been a small dot in the sky, but now the dot was growing bigger, imperceptibly if one watched it steadily, but clearly visible if one looked only sporadically. They were gaining.

"Keep up the good work, Maggie," Remo said. "When we go back to the hotel, I'll do you an extra good turn."

"Sorry, Yank," she said. "I'm in mourning for P.J. Kenny, the only man I ever loved."

"May he rot in peace," Remo said. "The only time I've ever beaten my own time." But he was glad he would not again enjoy Maggie. With his identity had come back his disciplines. Sex was one of them.

Both planes ate up the distance to Scambia but Remo's craft took bigger bites. It was only a minute behind Nemeroff now and up ahead they saw the island of Scambia, down in the cool blue waters of Mozambique. Nemeroff's helicopter began to lose altitude. Maggie followed suit.

They were over Scambia now, a drab little island, its monotonous landscape relieved only by nature with rocks and not by man with buildings. Ahead, they could see the only large building on the island, a blue stone structure, surrounded by mazes of gardens and pools. Nemeroff's helicopter was heading down for it. They could see it touch down on the grounds. Two. No, three men scurried from it, and began running.

Maggie increased her speed, barreling the helicopter down, and she touched down alongside the other craft only forty-five seconds after it had landed.

"Good show," Remo said. "Pip, pip and all that. If you Britishers weren't frigid, I think I could love you." A glance showed that Nemeroff's helicopter was empty. "Chiun," Remo said. "Get in and protect the president. The vice president is going to try to kill him. Maggie and I will go for the gold, to stop Nemeroff from getting it."

Before he finished speaking, Chiun was out on the grassy field, moving toward the front of the palace.

There, two uniformed guards stood at attention, their eyes carefully watching the helicopters, watching the people who had climbed from the two aircraft, now watching this old Oriental come skittering across the deep green grass at them. They had been given orders to let no one into the palace. Extreme security precautions, Vice President Asiphar himself had just told them.

Then Chiun was in front of them. They were moving to block him with their rifles and then he was not there. One guard turned to the other and said: "What happened to that old man?"

"I don't know," the other guard said. "Did you hear someone say 'excuse me'?"

"No, it couldn't be," said the first guard, and they watched again across the field as Remo and the girl headed for the east wing of the palace.

There was another guard inside on the first floor of the palace's central wing. He felt a tap on his shoulder and turned to see an old Oriental standing there. "The president. Where is he?" Chiun asked.

"What are you doing here?" the guard asked, which was the wrong thing to ask. A hand grabbed his waist, and ringers like knives poked their ways into clusters of nerves; the pain was agonizing.

"Fool. Where is your president?"

"At the head of the stairs," the man managed to gasp through his pain, and then he lapsed into unconsciousness.

Chiun glided up the stairs, his feet seeming not to move under the heavy robe. There were no guards outside the heavy double doors that obviously led to the president's office. Chiun pushed open the doors and stepped inside.

Across the room, President Dashiti worked at his desk, and he looked up as Chiun entered his field of vision. For a moment he was startled, then he said: "Forgive my staring. One is not always surprised at one's desk by Orientals in robes."

"In this world," Chiun said, "one should be surprised at nothing."

"True enough," the president said, his hand straying toward the signal button on his desk, to call the guards to escort this old lunatic out.

Chiun wagged a finger at him, naughty-naughty.

"I beg your indulgence, Mr. President. Men are coming to assassinate you."

Yes. Obviously a lunatic. But how did he get past the guards outside?

"I must ask you to leave," Dashiti said.

"Ask all you wish," Chiun said. "But I will stay and save you, even though you do not wish saving."

The President's finger moved closer to the alarm button.

Down the hall, Asiphar spoke to two men who stood in his small office.

"It is time," he said, "the baron has arrived." He turned from his window and looked at the men, both tall and European-looking.

"I have removed the guards. Just walk into his office and shoot him. I will follow at the sound of the shots and will confirm your story that others shot him and you attempted to stop them."

The two men smiled, the knowing smile of one professional to another.

"Now, go quickly. The guards may soon return."

The two men nodded and went out into the hall. Quickly they walked to the president's door. Asiphar stood in the doorway of his own office, watched them push back the heavy door and enter Dashiti's inner sanctum. Now to wait for the shots. Oh, yes. He would help them get away. Right to their final resting place. When he heard the shots, he would race into Dashiti's office. And what else could a loyal vice president do, except kill the men who had killed his president? What better way to gain for himself public support and approval?

He waited, and as the door closed behind the two assassins, he lifted the safety on his pistol.

Baron Isaac Nemeroff had not entered the castle. Instead, he had run to the outside wall of the east wing, where the sewer crew had been working for the last month.

The sewer foreman saw Nemeroff racing toward him across the open field in front of the palace and snapped to attention.

"Come," Nemeroff said, "we must proceed quickly."

The supervisor jumped down into the deep sewer trench that ran for fifty feet parallel to the east wall of the palace. Workers scattered to move out of the way as Nemeroff followed.

The supervisor pointed. At right angles from the trench, heading straight toward the palace wall was a tunnel, tall enough for a man to move through, while standing up. It stopped at the palace wall. The supervisor flashed a light at the wall. Nemeroff could see the crew's handiwork. During the last four weeks, they had quietly drilled into and removed the mortar holding the stones of the wall together.

"All it takes now," the supervisor said, "is a jolt with a jackhammer. The whole wall will open up."

"Then do it," Nemeroff said. "Timing is all, now." He waved to one of the men to back their truck to the edge of the trench. In minutes, Asiphar would be President. The president of a country without a dime; the world's pauper. There would be no other game in town, except Nemeroff.

The supervisor grabbed a jackhammer and went into the dark tunnel. After a moment, there came the terrific thump, thump, thump, so fast it was not a series of separate sounds but flooded the small tunnel with overpowering noise.

Then it stopped. Nemeroff heard the thump of stones falling onto a stone floor and rolling to a halt.

The supervisor came out of the dark to the trench-end of the tunnel where Nemeroff waited.

"It is done," he said.

Nemeroff brushed by him and went to the wall of the palace treasury room. The stones had been splintered and cracked. Some had fallen out. He pressed a hand against another stone. It fell easily, thumping on the floor of the dark room inside. Nemeroff began to push the stones free from the wall; they came loose like children's Styrofoam building blocks.

He pushed and pulled stones away until he had made a hole big enough to step through easily, then clambered inside.

It was a small room, perhaps only twenty feet square, but it was dark and it took Nemeroff's sun-squinted eyes moments to adjust to the darkness. Gradually, the room came into focus. At the far end was a heavy steel door, which he knew was electrified and on the other side of which stood a squad of guards.

And on pallets, all around the outside walls of the room, were stacked gold bullion, bar after bar, one hundred million dollars worth, the total wealth of the nation of Scambia.

Nemeroff giggled. Asiphar was in for a surprise. Talk about a president's hundred days. There would be Asiphar's hundred minutes. He would become president and the country would instantly become bankrupt. So? What was wrong with that? It happened to all African countries eventually. Nemeroff was just speeding up the process.

And soon — despite that Remo Williams and that Oriental and that woman — despite all them, the crime families of the world would have new leaders and they would listen when Nemeroff spoke. Scambia would still be under crime's flag.

And someday, the Russians and the Americans might want missile bases here. What if they were willing to pour the wealth of their lands into this godforsaken island? This room could be filled with gold again and again, and again and again Nemeroff could drain it.

He turned and called to his men. "Set up a line," he said. "Begin to pass out these bars. You, get in there and start," he called to the supervisor.

Still trailing the jackhammer behind him, the man came into the small treasury room — into its darkness — and then it was dark no longer. Suddenly the overhead lights glared and glinted sharply off the gold, bathing the room almost in sunlight. Nemeroff blinked sharply, squeezing his eyelids together. When he opened them, at the end of the room, sitting on a stack of bullion, was the British woman and the man he had known as P.J. Kenny.

The two gunmen entered the presidential office. The president's blue leather chair was turned away from them, facing the window. It rocked gently back and forth.

Both men held guns in their hands and one raised his, but the second man raised a hand in caution. Not at this distance. Wait.

They walked softly across the heavily-padded carpet to the President's desk.

They smiled at each other. A breeze. Walk up to him, one from each side. Two bullets in the head. No sweat.

They drew near the presidential chair. Their guns came up. The chair slowly swung around and smiling at them, looking from face to face, was not the President, but the wizened parchment face of an ancient Oriental.

In the corridor Asiphar waited. Then he heard two shots.

He unsnapped his holster and ran toward the President's office.

Inside the door, he stopped. The two gunmen stood alongside the President's chair, but their bodies were contorted and twisted. In the chair sat an aged Oriental in blue flowing robes, who looked at Asiphar as if he recognized him. He raised his hands toward Asiphar across the room, and as he released the two gunmen, they fell to the floor softly.

The old Oriental stood up. His eyes burned into Asiphar's. The vice president looked at the two dead men on the floor, first in horror, then in puzzlement. He looked up again at the old man, as if he would find an answer in the Oriental's face.

He reached for his pistol.

The old man said, "They missed," and then he was over the top of the desk, in the air, coming toward Asiphar, and the last words Asiphar heard in the world were: "But the Master of Sinanju does not miss."

He never got his gun from his holster. His heavy body hit the carpeted floor with no more sound than suet falling on a mattress.

From inside a closet door stepped President Dashiti. He looked at the two dead gunmen. At dead Asiphar. And then at Chiun.

"How may I repay you?" he said softly.

"By giving me some method of transportation home besides a helicopter."

Far away, as if from miles away, came the sound of tiny cracks. Chiun heard them; recognized them as shots. Wordlessly, he was gone from the President's office.

"Get him!" Nemeroff shouted. He stood aside and men poured through the tunnel into the treasury room.

Remo sat unconcernedly on the gold bars, humming.

Three men — four, then five — poured into the small room. They stood, waiting, as their supervisor, holding the jackhammer under his arm as if it were a rifle, advanced toward Remo and Maggie, his lips twisted in a thin smile.

Remo waited, then reached up a hand and flipped the switch, plunging the room into darkness again.

Nemeroff tried to see into the darkness, but could not.

Then the room was filled with the awful roar of a jackhammer, but as quickly as it started, it stopped. Then it started again, and there was a scream.

"Did you get him?" Nemeroff called.

"No Baron, he missed. My turn now." It was the voice of the American.

The dark room was illuminated briefly by the flashes of gunfire. In the stroboscopic pulses of light. Nemeroff watched an eerie tableau of death. The American held the jackhammer under his arm. Nemeroff's men fired at him. But he was never there. More shots. And then fewer. In the flashes of light, he saw that men were falling, screaming, struggling as they were impaled on the jackhammer like bugs.

Nemeroff fled.

He ran along the tunnel toward the sunlight. He jumped up out of the trench and broke in a dead run for the field, where his pilot had already begun to warm up the helicopter's engines.

In the treasury room, Remo dropped the jackhammer. There was no one left.

Through the dark, his cat's eyes looked toward Maggie, who still sat motionless, atop the pallet of gold.

"Maggie. You all right?"

"Yes."

"I'm going after Nemeroff." He headed toward the sunlight. Maggie got to her feet and followed him, trailing at her side the .45 caliber automatic she still had not fired.

Nemeroff was already in the helicopter and it was lifting from the ground when Remo came out into the sunlight. He heard Maggie stumble behind him and turned to help her.

Behind him, the helicopter rose, and then swooped toward them. Remo pulled Maggie up onto the street next to the sewer trench, then turned. Overhead, roaring at them came the helicopter.

Dammit, he thought, Smith'll bust my balls if I let him get away.

Then shots came from the helicopter, plinking the pavement around Remo, and he heard one thump softly next to him. As he turned, Maggie fell onto the roadway. Blood poured from a wound in her chest. The .45 dropped from her hand.

The helicopter hovered overhead, thirty feet off the ground, and shots rained from it, showering the ground with lead, as Nemeroff fired at Remo.

Remo ignored him and looked at Maggie. She smiled once and died.

He picked up the .45, wheeled and fired. He missed. Nemeroff, seeing the weapon in Remo's hands, remembering his marksmanship told his pilot to fly off.

The bird hovered, then its motor changed pitch, as it began to pull away.

Chiun came around the corner of the palace. He saw Remo, holding the .45 with both hands at arm's length, squeezing a shot at the helicopter which was moving away.

It was out of .45 range now.

Chiun ran up and took the pistol from Remo's hands.

"The Jesus nut," Remo shouted. "It holds the rotor blades on. Got to get it."

Chiun shook his head sadly. "You will never learn," he said. "The target that lives is the target that gives itself to the marksman."

Almost casually, he aimed the automatic in the direction of the fleeing helicopter. He extended his right arm, holding the .45 and gently the barrel of the gun transcribed a circle in air, and then a smaller circle, and yet a smaller circle.

"Shoot, for Christ's sake. They'll be in Paris," Remo said. The helicopter was two hundred yards away now, hopelessly out of range.

And still Chiun's arm rotated the .45 in ever-tightening concentric circles, zoning in, and then he squeezed the trigger. Once.

He dropped the gun, turned his back on the helicopter, and knelt alongside the girl.

He had missed. He must have missed. The range was too far; the target too small. Then, as Remo watched, the helicopter pitched forward, and then it dropped, plummeting, like a rock, and there was a flash of light, and a split-second later an explosion as the aircraft crashed into the rocky soil of Scambia.

Chiun stood up. "She is dead, my son," he said.

"I know," Remo said. "You got the pilot."

"I know," Chiun said. "Did you doubt I would?"

"Not for a moment," Remo said. "Let's go. Smith owes us a vacation. I need to rest."

"You need to practice the back elbow thrust," Chiun said.

THE END

EXCERPT

If you enjoyed *Summit Chase*, maybe you'll like *Murder's Shield*, too. It's the ninth Destroyer novel, now available in paperback and as an ebook.

Murder's Shield

HIS NAME WAS REMO and as he stood on the platform high in the darkened tent, he felt that his body was one with the forces of nature and he was the depth of all human strength.

The animal smells of the empty arena below were strong eighty feet above the sawdust. The outside breeze slapped at the tent. It was cold in that little high pocket where he stood and the swinging bar felt cold as death under his hands as he flipped it back in a long smooth arc.

"Has he done it yet?" said someone down below.

"You have not been paid to witness but to provide this area which you are not using now. Begone," responded a squeaky Oriental voice below.

"But there are no safety nets."

"You were not asked to supervise safety," came the creaky Oriental voice.

"But I gotta see this. There's no lights up there. He's at the top of the high trapeze with no lights."

"One finds seeing things difficult when one's face is buried in the ground."

"Are you trying to threaten me, Pops? C'mon, old man."

Remo stopped the bar. He yelled down to the cavernous arena.

"Chiun. Leave him alone. And you, buddy, if you don't get out of here, you don't get paid."

"What's it any skin off your nose? You're committing suicide anyway. Besides, I already got my money."

"Look," yelled Remo. "Just get away from that little old man. Please."

"The noble elderly gentleman with the wise eyes," added Chiun, lest the circus owner be confused by Remo's description.

"I ain't botherin' no one."

"You are bothering me," said Chiun.

"Well, Pops, that's the way it goes. I'm sitting down right here."

Suddenly there was a piercing scream at the floor of the tent. Remo saw a large balloon of a figure pitch forward and land on its face. It did not move.

"Chiun. That guy just wanted to sit down. You better not have done anything serious."

"When one removes garbage, one does not do anything serious."

"He'd better be alive."

"He never was alive. I could smell hamburger meat on his foul breath. You could smell the meat miles away. He was not alive."

"Well, his heart better be beating."

"It's beating," came the response from below. "And I am aging, waiting to see the simplest of skills, the meager accomplishments of my great and intense years of training, some small proof that the best years of my life have not been wasted on a dullard."

"I mean beating so that he will wake up, not just the twitching of a stiff."

"Do you wish to come down here and kiss him?"

"All right, all right."

"And let us attempt decent form this time, please."

Remo threw the bar out. He knew that Chiun could see him as if stage lights flooded the darkness at the top of the tent. The eye was a muscle and to see in darkness was only an adjustment of that muscle, which could be trained as any other muscle could. It was almost a decade before that Chiun had first told him this, told him that most men go to the grave using less than ten per cent of their skills, muscles, coordination and nerves. "One must only look at the grasshopper," Chiun had said, "or the ant to see energy properly used. Man has forgotten this use. I will remind you."

Remind him he had, in years of training that had more than once brought Remo to the threshold of mind-shattering pain, past the limits of what he had thought a human body could do. And always there were new limits.

"Get on with it," came Chiun's voice.

Remo caught the bar and threw it again. He felt its presence swing out across the tent. Then his body took over. The toes flipped and the hands were forward and he was in space, rising to the apex before the fall, and at the apex, the bar which his senses perceived in the darkness was there in his hands. Up he swung, flipping his body in somersaults just above the swinging bar within the frame of the two wires holding the bar. One. Two.

Three. Four. Then catch the bar with the knees and balance. Hands at sides, knees on bar swinging backward, again to the apex and then, like a chess piece, topple backward, free of the bar, free of any support, falling, down to the sawdust, a lead force dropping to earth, and no movement, head first, not a muscle moving, not even a vagrant thought in the mind. Bang. The cat-fast center of the body forward, feet out, catch the ground, go down to it, perfect even decompression.

On the feet, stand up straight, weight perfectly balanced.

"Perfect," thought Remo. "I was perfect this time. Even Chiun must admit it. As good as any Korean ever. As good as good Chiun, because his was perfection."

Remo strolled over to the aged Korean in the flowing white, golden-bordered robe.

"I think it came off fairly well," Remo said with feigned casualness.

"What?" said Chiun.

"The World Series. What do you think I was talking about?" said Remo.

"Oh, that," said Chiun.

"That," said Remo.

"That was proof that if you have someone of the quality of the Master of Sinanju, you can get a reasonable performance occasionally. Even from a white man."

"Reasonable?" Remo yelled. "Reasonable? That was perfect. That was perfection and I did it. If it wasn't perfect, what was wrong? Tell me, what was wrong?"

"It's chilly in here. Let us go."

"Name one thing any Master of Sinanju could have done better."

"Show less pride because pride is flaw."

"I mean, up on the bar," Remo persisted.

"I see our friend is moving. See how well I kept my promise on his staying alive?"

"Chiun, admit it. Perfection."

"Does my saying perfection make it perfection? If that is required, then the act itself was less than perfection. Therefore," said Chiun with a high happy note in his voice, "I must say that it was less than perfect."

The circus owner groaned and rose to his feet.

"What happened?" he asked.

"I decided not to try any tricks in the dark and climbed down," Remo said.

"You ain't getting your money back. You rented the place. If you didn't do your tricks, it ain't my fault. Anyway, you're lucky. Nobody ever did a four-somersault. Nobody."

"I guess you're right," Remo said.

The circus owner shook his head. "What happened to me?"

"One of your seats collapsed," said Remo.

"Where? Which one? They look good to me."

"This one over here," said Remo, touching the metal bottom of the seat nearest to Chiun.

When the circus owner saw the crack appear before his eyes, he attributed it to the fall he had taken. Otherwise he would have had to believe that this nut who'd chickened out on the high-wire tricks, had actually cracked the bottom of a metal seat with his hand. And he wasn't about to believe that of anyone.

Remo put on his street clothes over his dark tights, a pair of flared blue flannel pants and a clean blue shirt with just enough collar not to appear stodgy. His dark hair was trimmed short and his angular features were handsome enough to belong to a movie star. But the dark eyes said that this was not a movie star. The eyes did not communicate; they absorbed, and looking into them gave some people the uneasy feeling of staring into a cave. He was of average build and only his thick wrists belied any superior strength.

"Didja forget your wristwatch?" asked the circus owner.

"No," said Remo. "I don't wear one any more."

"Too bad," said the owner. "Mine's broken and I've got an appointment."

"It's three forty-seven and thirty seconds," said Remo and Chiun in unison. The owner looked puzzled.

"You guys are kidding, right?"

"Right," said Remo.

Seconds later, outside the tent, the owner was surprised to find that the time was three forty-eight. But the two men were not around to be asked how they could tell time without wristwatches. They were in a car on their way to a motel room on the outskirts of Fort Worth, Texas, zipping along a highway strewn with beer cans and the bodies of dogs — the victims of Texas drivers who believe head-on collisions are just another form of brakes.

"Something is bothering you, my son," said Chiun.

Remo nodded. "I think I'm going to be on the wrong side."

Chiun's frail parchment face became puzzled.

"Wrong side?"

"Yes, I think I'm going in on the wrong side this time." His voice was glum.

"What is a wrong side? Will you cease to work for Doctor Smith?"

"Look, you know I can't explain to you who we work for."

"I've never cared," said Chiun. "What difference would it make?"

"It does make a difference, dammit. Why do you think I do what I do?"

"Because you are a pupil of the Master of Sinanju and you perform your assassin's art because that is what you are. The flower gives to the bee and the bee makes honey. The river flows and mountains sit content and sometimes rumble. Each is what he is. And you, Remo, are a student in the House of Sinanju despite the fact that you are white."

"Dammit, Chiun, I'm an American, and I do what I do for other reasons. And now, they've told me to get up to a peak right away, and then I find out I'm going in against the good guys."

"Good guys? Bad guys? Are you living in a fairy tale, my son? You sound like the little children yelling things in the street or your president on the picture box. Have you not learned of our teaching? Good guys, bad guys! There are killing points, nerve points, hearts and lungs and eyes and feet and hands and balance. There are no good guys and bad guys. If there were, would armies have to wear uniforms to identify themselves?"

"You wouldn't understand, Chiun."

"I understand that the poor of the village of Sinanju eat, because the Master of Sinanju serves a master who pays. The food of one tastes just as sweet as the food of another. It is food. You have not learned fully, but you will." Chiun shook his head sadly. "I have given you perfection, as you demonstrated this afternoon, and now you act like a white man."

"So you admit it was perfect?"

"What good is perfection in the hands of a fool? It is a precious emerald buried in a dung heap."

And with that, Chiun was silent, but Remo paid no attention to his silence. He was angry, almost as angry as he had been that day a decade before when he had recovered from his public execution, waking up in Folcroft Sanitarium on Long Island Sound.

Remo Williams had been framed for a murder he did not commit, and then publicly executed in an electric chair that did not work. When he recovered, they told him that they had needed a man who did not exist to act as the killer arm for an agency set up outside the U.S. Constitution to preserve that Constitution from organized crime, revolutionaries, and from all who would overthrow the nation. The crime-fighting organization was CURE, and only four men knew of it: The President of the United States, Dr. Harold Smith, head of CURE, the recruiter, and now Remo. And the recruiter had killed himself to prevent himself from talking, telling Remo that "America is worth a life." Then there were only three who knew.

That was the moment when Remo decided to take the job. And for a decade, he thought he had long since buried the Remo Williams he used to be — a simple, foot-slogging patrolman on the Newark police force. It was so long ago that he had been a cop; and that cop had died in the electric chair.

So Remo had thought...until now. But now he realized that the policeman had not died in the electric chair. Patrolman Remo Williams still lived. His stomach told him. It was churning at the thought of his new assignment; having to kill fellow cops.

ABOUT THE AUTHORS

WARREN MURPHY (1933 – 2015) was born in Jersey City, where he worked in journalism and politics until launching the **Destroyer** series with Richard Sapir in 1971. A screenwriter (*Lethal Weapon II, The Eiger Sanction*) as well as a novelist, Murphy's work won a dozen national awards, including multiple Edgars and Shamuses. He was a lecturer at many colleges and universities; his lessons on writing a novel are available on his website, WarrenMurphy.com. A Korean War veteran, some of Murphy's many hobbies included golf, mathematics, opera, and investing. He served on the board of the Mystery Writers of America, and was a member of the Screenwriters Guild, the Private Eye Writers of America, the International Association of Crime Writers, and the American Crime Writers League. He has five children: Deirdre, Megan, Brian, Ardath, and Devin.

RICHARD BEN SAPIR was a New York native who worked as an editor and in public relations, before creating *The Destroyer* series with Warren Murphy. Before his untimely death in 1987, Sapir had also penned a number of thriller and historical mainstream novels, best known of which were *The Far Arena, Quest* and *The Body*, the last of which was made recently into a film. The New York Times book review section called him "a brilliant professional."

Made in the USA
Las Vegas, NV
02 June 2021

24091998R00089